BLACK MAGIC

A HUTCHINSON NOVELLA

BLACK MAGIC

General Editor: Frank Delaney

NIGEL WILLIAMS

BLACK MAGIC

WITH ILLUSTRATIONS BY
JULEK HELLER

HUTCHINSON

LONDON   MELBOURNE   AUCKLAND   JOHANNESBURG

Series Design by Craig Dodd

© Text Nigel Williams 1988
© Illustrations Julek Heller 1988

First published in 1988 by Hutchinson, an imprint of Century Hutchinson Ltd,
Brookmount House, 62–65 Chandos Place, London WC2N 4NW

Century Hutchinson Australia Pty Ltd
PO Box 496, 16–22 Church Street, Hawthorn, Victoria 3122, Australia

Century Hutchinson Group New Zealand Ltd
PO Box 40–086, Glenfield, Auckland 10, New Zealand

Century Hutchinson Group South Africa (Pty) Ltd
PO Box 337, Bergvlei 2012, South Africa

British Library Cataloguing in Publication Data

Williams, Nigel, *1948–*
  Black magic.
  I. Title
  823'.914[F]
ISBN 0–09–170950–5 4

Typeset in Monophoto Photina by
Vision Typesetting, Manchester

Printed in Great Britain by
Butler & Tanner Ltd, Frome and London

To Suzan

A HUTCHINSON NOVELLA

ONE

My father died in the Spring of 1984, in a hospital in West London. I remember the daffodils were just out and, though I'm not normally the sort of person who notices flowers, when I was visiting him I could not take my eyes off the scattering of yellow and green on the hospital lawn that lay between his ward and the suburban street beyond. It rained often when I was there. There was sleet, too, and cold, easterly winds that seemed to mock the flowers' gesture of renewal.

Everything about that Spring was confusing. The heat in the hospital, the cold outside, the physical resurrection of the earth on the other side of the glass, and, in the lifeless womb of the hospital, the kind of death that seemed utterly final, since I had chosen not to believe in the Christian faith that was, in name anyway, my father's. He was too intelligent a man to believe anything completely.

It was that Spring that I started to tell my children stories. Like flowers, stories were, before that time, things I was aware of, *approved* of, in a dim sort of way, but not things that I felt I understood. I would not have been able to sit with any of my three sons, with my arms round them, and simply make up a tale to amuse them, the way my father had done when I was a child. I

1

even felt too self-conscious to take a book down from the shelves to read to them. My voice sounded hollow, false. I left that sort of thing to my wife.

And yet, while my father was dying, inch by inch, his face turning whiter and whiter until it was the colour of the clouds I could see from his window, I started to tell them stories.

Not just at bedtime.

When we were out in the car, on trips to Sainsbury's, when we were walking together in Richmond Park, when we were in the bath, I found myself, time and again, gaining their attention with phrases and formulas remembered from my own, forgotten, childhood.

'Once upon a time . . .

'Years ago there was a . . .'

'Listen, listen, this is a *true* story and it actually happened. . .'

Sometimes they were stories of goblins and giants. One was a story about a boy called Toast, who discovered a highly secret passage underneath a secret Lavatory in Richmond Park (small boys enjoy anything to do with lavatories). One was a story about a penguin who was taught to speak English by a Norwegian explorer called Bjölli and who, disguised as a short person in evening dress, won various showbiz awards. There was a story called 'The Unpleasant Frog' and a rather disappointing tale entitled 'The Disgusting Rabbit'. I could not understand, even as I told them, where the stories came from or quite what they might mean, but my children followed all of them, wide-eyed. They interrupted, asked questions, laughed, contradicted me. They didn't care whether the stories were good or bad. What they liked was the *activity*.

When I told them the stories were true they would watch me with small, suspicious eyes, trying to catch me out. I told them about a man called Widderkins, who had a head shaped like a corkscrew, and they believed the story (or said they did) right up to the point at which he discovered oil while trying to do a headstand in the front garden of his home in Finchley.

'There ith no oil in Finchley', said my middle son, Paul, a small, precise eight-year-old.

'There was,' I said. 'Years and years ago.'

'When?' he said. 'When woth there oil?'

At such moments they knew they had me on the run. I had to be resourceful and energetic and positive to make these imaginary worlds seem as real and necessary as the resurrection I so wanted for my father. And I found, to my surprise, that I was able to be all these things.

My wife didn't like it.

Earlier that year, she had been to Greenham Common. Not to stay; just to look. The experience had changed her. I thought it had simply made her more the way she was already, but she said it was more than that.

She had driven round the perimeter fence with a friend, she said. When she told me about the landscape it sounded as barbaric and weird as anything in the stories I was telling the children. 'It's like black magic', she said. 'There's this huge black fence and it goes on for *miles* and behind it are these alien soldiers and the place is like some wicked castle. And outside are the women, the *women*. . . .'

She kept talking about 'the women'. I didn't want to hear about them or the 'wonderful work' they were doing. I didn't want to hear how purposeful and brave and persecuted they were, or how they were going to save us from death and the Americans. The only kind of death I wanted to talk about was my father's. Maybe, I told her, the women were right, and because of what was happening behind the barbed wire at Greenham we were all going to die, but in the end, I said, we all die, and my father was dying now. Not next year or the year after that. Not as a result of SALT 2 or the Cruise Missiles but because he was mortal and his

3

time had come, as cruelly and unexpectedly as it will for all of us.

But, all that Spring, she talked about the women and I talked about my father.

I don't want to make it sound as if she ranted at me. She never rants. And neither were her opinions as neatly formed as I have made them sound. I suppose I caricature her only because I don't quite understand her. My lack of curiosity about what she does when she walks out of our front door might be construed as lack of interest; it isn't. She has the right to do what she wants to do without telling me about it. Even attempting to describe her feels like a worse kind of treachery than the sort I am seen to be practising here, easily covered with the appropriate story. But, if only to clear myself of the charge of unconcern, I will try to say how she is.

My wife is a clever, beautiful woman of nearly forty. She has the face (people say) of a peasant Madonna. What they don't say about her – although some of them may think it – is that her cleverness is of the kind that makes people uncomfortable. It is not a decorative kind of intelligence, but a bizarre Irish bluntness (she was born in Dublin). Jane sounds as if she is describing the world about her in a brusque, housewifely way; it is only when you think about what she is saying that you realize that there is something that baffles her about her life. That, anyway, is how she struck me that Spring, when I was telling the children stories.

She said there was no truth in them. She didn't mean it the way the children did. She meant the stories didn't tell her what she wanted to hear. She didn't like the male jokes, the references to lavatories, and she hated the princesses and witches I put into the stories.

'You're making them hate women,' she said.

My middle son, Paul, who lisps with a curious, implacable confidence, who likes football and standing on his head in the

4

front garden, professes to hate women, or rather girls. Women are merely adults to him and so, like all adults, second-class individuals who demand first-class status. But girls. 'Girls . . . girls,' he says, 'try to kiss you and snog with you and play kiss-chase with you.' And when Jane says 'But I'm a girl . . .' he says, 'No, you're not. You're my Mummy. And I love you.'

I made up one story about a boy who hated girls so much he put them on an island in the middle of the sea. In the story the girls became as fierce and strong as any boy and when, years later, the boy was washed ashore on their island they roasted him over a slow fire and ate him.

'You could say,' I said to Jane, 'it was a punishment for his sexist attitude.'

Jane is a teacher and she constantly uses words like 'racist' and 'sexist'. To me, the words don't have much to do with the things they purport to describe. What they describe is so awful and cruel and pointless that these limp little words, shards of a half-formed ideology, do not do them justice.

After a while she stopped wanting me to touch her. Once, she had said, I didn't touch her enough. Now, when we made love, she offered herself to me briefly, seriously, privately, as if she were frightened of losing the boundaries of herself. As if she didn't trust me.

She was right not to trust me.

That Spring I had begun an affair with a singer from New York. She was from somewhere else before New York (it may even have been England) but her publicity described her as a New Yorker and, since I was writing it, I went along with the publicity. I went along with most things about her – her soprano voice, her close-cropped black hair and her pear-shaped behind. I got a great deal of pleasure from my work that Spring.

There was another man in New York, she said, but that didn't bother me.

I started to tell the story I am about to recall four weeks before my father died. It began for me (and for them) one evening after a trip to Greenwich to see the Maritime Museum. Sam, the five-year-old, had rolled all the way down the steep hill on which the Observatory sits, asking, with delight, as he sat up, 'What country is this?' I wanted to answer, 'This is Illyria', but Jane, who takes the business of their education very seriously, began to explain the difference between *towns* and *suburbs* and *counties* and *countries*.

She was practically on to postal districts when I said, 'It's in England. We're in England. That's all he needs to know.'

'All?' said Jane.' 'Is it *all?*'

Then we were started on colonialism and jingoism and what being English meant and how being English was so much less vibrant and meaningful and liable to get you into the colour supplements than being Peruvian or Chinese.

I said: 'I'm English and I'm glad I'm English and I think we should teach them to love what they are. What's so wrong with being English?' Which led us on, I am afraid, to politics. By the time we had reached the car Jane had announced her intention of going home on her own. She didn't like any of us, she said; she couldn't stand to be in the company of men any longer. Men were the only cruel things in the world. *They're responsible for the wars and the famines and the bombs that will come and wipe us all out. Men, with their ghastly conceit and lust for knowing things and showing off about them.* I suppose she said this because I pride myself on being precise in argument and not allowing my feelings to interfere with my reason; even when discussing machines that may end in the extinction of the planet.

'Fine,' I said, 'walk home. Go and find some women and live with them if you want. . . .'

I piled the children into the car. Before I had time to consider what I was doing I had driven fifty yards down the street, and the children had started to shout at me as well. Sam began to cry. I was about to turn and drive back to her, but before I could do so I saw, in the driving mirror, that she was walking briskly away, as if to some pre-arranged meeting. She looked back once, briefly, then turned down towards the Thames and vanished from sight. I laid my head on the steering wheel.

'Wot'th the matter?' said Paul.

Tom, his elder brother, was unaware of what was going on. Through the day he had been reading a book called *The Dungeon of Destiny*. From time to time, as the book instructed him, he would take out a dice, throw it, scribble messages to himself on a piece of paper, then leaf through the pages of the book to find out whether he was about to be awarded the sword of power or be eaten alive by crocodiles. The book's cover said, 'In this story you are the hero', but Tom didn't look like a hero when he was reading it. He looked like a poetaster, a young man in a trance.

'Mum's cross,' I said.

'Why?' said Paul.

'People get cross,' I replied.

I turned the car round and drove back towards the river. For some reason I was sure that was where she had gone but, although I followed the next road that might lead me to the edge of the stream, I could not see her anywhere. *She's gone down a side turning*, I thought, *a path. She's sitting, hunched up on a seat, staring at the Thames, a sullen expression on her face.*

I drove the children home.

The five-year-old had stopped crying but he didn't say much. He looked as if he had finally worked out what country he was in, but decided he didn't like the language, customs or kinship system one little bit. He sat, his huge head swivelled to one side, as the Spring townscape slid past.

I thought about my father, and how he had driven me and my brother home from trips very like this one. I felt as if my father were stepping into me. Taking over my body. His broad shoulders were pushing into mine and his duck feet grinding their way forward into my shoes. I was holding the steering wheel the way he used to hold it, and turning my feet down the way he used to do.

'Old Bignose,' I could almost hear my brother say (that was his name for him), 'looks as if he has a truncheon stuffed up his arse.' Only now Old Bignose was me.

I didn't want to be him. It reminded me that I, too, was going to die. I didn't like being in charge of these children. I wanted to be the one laughing at authority, not the one who represented it.

After a while, Paul said: 'Tell uth a thtory.'

So I did. And this is the story I started to tell them.

TWO

'Once upon a time,' I said, as we drove up through New Cross, past empty cafés, past bleak, military-looking pubs and blocks of flats whose windows were broken or boarded up, 'once upon a time there was a black magician and nobody liked him.

They liked his brother, the white magician, who specialised in potions to relieve arthritis and tablets to make you happy. Even though the white magician's happy tablets simply made you want to go to the lavatory, and the side-effects of his arthritis potion could be so unpleasant that most people preferred their creaking joints.

The black magician's magic worked. That was what people didn't like about it.

It wasn't spectacular stuff. He had never turned anyone into a toad, although he had once done something unpleasant *to* a toad; he had never disappeared or caused high winds or storms or long droughts. He specialised in low-grade black magic. Spells to make you fart. Ritual methods of forcing you to eat school dinners. Rules designed to create a poor performance in examinations.

He lived in a small, scruffy hut on the outskirts of a large town, and, when people came to see him, which I am afraid they did   9 rather frequently, they would walk past, whistling, as if they were on their way to somewhere else. Only when they were sure the coast was clear would they turn round and scuttle furtively up his crooked front path, hammer on his front door and slip inside to collect the pills, the lotion, or magic formula, that would guarantee their granny's premature baldness or the gruesome death of a pet.

He made a great deal of money, though he never spent it.

He was not a happy man. This was not because he had scruples (he had absolutely none whatsoever) but because he was unable to do as much harm as he would have liked. He practised low-

grade black magic not out of choice, but because he lacked the skills to do otherwise. He did not, he told himself, *wish* to spend the rest of his life splitting up happily married couples or working out spells to induce stage fright in celebrated actresses. He wanted to do something *really* wicked.

And yet, like many evil people, he had very little imagination. Sometimes, when the last of his customers had gone, he would lie on the floor of his scullery, drum his heels on the tiles and howl with frustration. He felt sure that he had it in him to do something absolutely unspeakable and disgusting, but he could not, for the life of him, think what it was.

One day, as he was staring out at the road that ran past his cottage, he saw a spotty youth stroll past, glance over at the tumbledown roof, the crazy chimney, the dusty, cracked windows, and hesitate. *A customer!* And the mean expression on the boy's face gave him an idea.

He would do something vile to the white magician.

Although they were brothers they did not speak to each other. Or rather, the black magician did not speak to the white magician. The white magician was always coming round to his brother's house and offering to clean it for him, or suggesting they visit their widowed mother who lived in a wood some miles away. But the black magician (who did not speak to his mother either) would sneer and pout and turn his back.

He would steal something from his brother's house. He would. . . .

Once again his small malicious brain gave out on him. He could not yet think quite *what* he would do. He would steal round to his brother's house, on a hill on the other side of town, and, as soon as he saw the dense mass of roses, the exquisitely wild orchard or the sickeningly clean windows of his brother's work-room he would know.

He put on an old black coat, a pair of bedroom slippers, his black magician's hat (a bit like a bus conductor's, only with a peak all the way round and a spike in the middle) and went out of the back door and across the fields, leaving his first customer of the day trying to pluck up the nerve to knock on the door of an empty house.

He was beginning to feel almost cheerful.

On his way through the town, past the market square, the cathedral, the unpretentious river and the municipal gardens, he bowed elaborately to all the local people, who pretended not to know him. This did not prevent the black magician calling out to the mayor, the town clerk or the head of the police department, for he knew something shameful about all of them. Even the local priest occasionally visited his shack, requesting a potion for a purpose so disgusting I dare not tell you what it was.

But the children of the town turned their faces away when the black magician passed and, though he smiled at them, they did not answer, for they were afraid of him.

As he reached the outskirts of the town and passed by the houses of the wealthy citizens, with huge, high-walled gardens, their dogs howled and snarled at him. Soon, however, he had left the last of the town behind him and he was climbing the white road, through fields of graceful, green corn, that led to his brother's house.

The white magician had built his own house, with the aid of a handbook. His brother was accustomed to say to anyone who would listen that a gorilla could have done a better job. The door was at an angle of forty-five degrees to the windows, while the windows were at an angle of thirty degrees to the floor; the floor itself sloped downwards at an angle of fifteen or twenty degrees, so that all the furniture collected in a heap in the far right hand corner of the kitchen. The drains didn't work, and, when anyone knocked at the front door, the upstairs lavatory flushed of its own accord.

And yet – there was a pleasant air about the place. Perhaps it was the rough white plaster that faced the outer walls. Perhaps it was the dark bundles of thatch that sat squarely on the roof. Or the huge picture windows of the white magician's workroom, facing out to the south. For it was here that you could always see him, bowed over his books, occasionally looking out over the peaceful landscape with such sweetness in his eye that the building seemed to have gathered round him, like harmony on a tune.

The black magician spied him at the window and, before his brother had a chance to see *him*, dived off the path and wriggled up through the growing corn like some agitated poisonous snake. He would spy on his brother a little first, he decided, as the morning sun burned his back. He would find out what the stupid, smug, sanctimonious, stuck-up swine was doing. Then he would spoil it.

13

Grinning downwards into the rich black soil, the evil magician squirmed on through the corn. From time to time he looked up at the window and often saw his brother move from his work-table further into the room, out of sight. A moment later he would walk back into view. Sometimes he raised his arms and shook his hands violently, then he would purse his lips, inflate his cheeks and push out through the rounded O of his mouth. Once the black magician saw him bend over something on the table, and to his surprise it seemed to him as if his brother were on the verge of speaking to – to what? And why?

"*Because*", said the black magician to himself, "*he thinks some good will come of it.*

'We'll see about that."

THREE

'When he finally saw what the white magician was on the verge
of addressing, the black magician was overjoyed. He had to crawl
up to the left of the house, towards the crest of the little hill at the
edge of the cornfield, but the journey was, he thought, well worth
it.

The white magician was bending over a small grey pebble.

That, in the black magician's view, proved that his brother had
gone barking mad. As a practising magician he had, of course,
heard of people talking to domestic furniture, usually with some
results, but a pebble!

The pebble was lying on some papers in the middle of his
brother's work-table. The white magician kept on performing the
same sequence of actions. He would bend over the object, open
his mouth as if he was about to say something, then rise up, puff
out his cheeks, raise his arms, shake his hands violently, and back
away into the room. Shaking his hands and puffing out his
cheeks, the black magician remembered, was something his
brother always did when he was trying to stop himself from doing
something he had been told not to do.

The way the white magician backed into the room confirmed
this view. As he stepped backwards he had a hurt, pleading

expression on his face, and, when he reached the far wall, he almost fell against it, as if he were trying to push himself away from the object on the table. But while he was squirming into the wall, like a pig trying to scratch itself, the white magician's eyes never once left the pebble. It seemed to fascinate him. And in his eyes was a look the black magician had only seen once before.

'He looks,' said the black magician to himself, 'just the way he did when Old Bignose died.' Old Bignose was his name for his father, whose real name was not of course Old Bignose or anything like it, but Herbert. At the thought of his father the black magician snarled quietly to himself. His brother was still pressed against the far wall, his face marked with fear and horror.

The black magician quite liked that. He often used to say that he would travel miles for a bit of fear and horror. The thing he most enjoyed in life was the sight of people in distress, and, though ideally they should be children, close relatives were a good substitute. He frequently hung around the edges of funerals, peering at the weeping relatives of the dead, and, if there were an accident, he was often first on the scene. He would take up a position behind a nearby rock or tree, and settle down, usually with sandwiches and a hot drink of some kind, to take in the screams of the wounded.

But as he watched, to *his* distress, the expression of fear and horror on his brother's face was replaced by the kind of smile the black magician most hated. It was as if his brother had caught sight of something so . . . well, so *beautiful* that it gave out a light, brighter and sweeter than that of the sun.

The black magician did not like the word *beautiful*. When he said it to himself (he was so lacking in imagination he had to speak his thoughts out loud, to check that he was actually thinking) he tried to put inverted commas round it, or say it in a Scottish accent, or in some way to disguise the awful, embarrassing, naked truth of what the word meant. But there was something about words like *beautiful*, even if you pronounced them "byoodifool" and hiccupped while saying them, that brought his face out in a hot flush.

Love was another word like that, and *peace* and. . . .

The black magician shook himself. "If I carry on like this," he said, "I'll have an epileptic fit." He concentrated hard on the word *spite* and wriggled a little closer to the picture window. He wanted to hear what his brother had to say to this pebble, if he ever got around to saying it. Knowing his brother as he did, he decided the white magician was probably asking it the secret of the Universe. At this thought the black magician began to giggle uncontrollably. He was of the opinion that if anyone knew the secret of the Universe it would almost certainly be a human being and, most probably, a human being with an academic qualification of some kind. He himself had once nearly gone to university but had been discovered cheating in one of the exams. His defence, that cheating was the highest form of intellectual skill, was not successful.

The black magician was about to scurry back down the hill and get some witnesses to his brother's deranged behaviour and was, indeed, wondering how the white magician would look in a straitjacket, and what sort of unpleasant treatment could be prescribed for him, when something extraordinary happened. The white magician bent down to the pebble, whispered to it, and the pebble started to hum.

It made the kind of noise that a top makes when spinning as fast as it is able, only the noise was at a much higher pitch and very much louder. It was impossible to tell, from where the black magician was standing, if the pebble *was* actually rotating at quite incredible speed and, if it was rotating, whether the rotation was causing the noise, or the noise the rotation.

There was heat, too, and a curious, sweet smell that gave promise of almost unbearable pleasure. But the heat and the scent were not quite that. They merely *looked* like heat and scent. And, as even as he said this to himself, the black magician quarrelled with the very thought. How was it possible to *see* heat or smell? Or, for that matter, to hear movement? Or to feel the rotation of a distant object? And yet this is what he thought he saw, felt and heard, so that he was no longer sure of whether the pebble was actually a pebble or was, by some magic, changing into something else in front of his very eyes.

18   Whatever was going on, however, the black magician could

see that it was powerful stuff. And he wanted a piece of it.

The pebble had now stopped humming, and the white magician was slumped over his work table, his head in his hands. He seemed suddenly exhausted. His brother crawled closer to the picture window. When he was about five yards away he heard the sounds of snoring.

The white magician was asleep.

The black magician straightened up or, rather, performed a series of movements that would have straightened him if he had been shaped differently, and walked up to the window. The pebble was lying on the table, inches away from his brother's nose. The black magician looked at his brother's mane of white hair, his bushy moustache, and his eyes, as black and lively as a lemur's. And then he noticed that the front door was wide open.

The white magician was fond of saying that he owned nothing worth stealing. His brother had once stolen a frying pan from him; the white magician had never noticed that it had gone, and

when asked about it said he vaguely remembered having a frying pan but could not for the life of him think what it was that he did with it when he had it.

His brother crept in through the open door, scooped up the pebble and as many of the white magician's papers as he could carry, and scurried out through the door. He ran until the white house could be seen no more, and only then did he slacken his pace. Even then from time to time he would glance nervously over his shoulder, as if he suspected someone of following him. Once he stopped and made a half-hearted attempt at flying. He rose about three feet in the air, wobbled precariously and fell with a bump to the ground, hurting his ankle as he did so. But as he limped through the outer streets of the town he was smiling to himself.

He might not have been a brilliant magician but he knew a magic pebble when he saw one.'

FOUR

Why did I choose a magic pebble that afternoon? There's a poem by Zbigniew Herbert about a pebble, but I don't think it was that that gave me the idea.

Jane and I met in the Geological Museum. I was a serious person in those days and I spent my time when I wasn't studying wandering round London on my own. I wanted to be a writer. Not just any kind of writer but someone who wrote long, absorbing novels, with a serious purpose. I thought, then, that fiction could change the way people think and feel. Could make them more moral. Well, I was young. Maybe it was that.

In the Geological Museum I sat for hours, looking at the rocks – the quartz, the graphite, the coal. I think I liked the quietness of the things, their permanence, and sometimes when I was there I'd take out a notebook and scribble. Outlines of stories, scraps of dialogue, sometimes cartoons.

I was there one rainy afternoon in February, scribbling, when I became aware of a girl with long blonde hair and a wide Irish face. She was standing above me looking at my notebook, rather in the way a commuter might spy on a fellow traveller's newspaper. I looked up. She smiled.

'Are you a scientist?' she said.

'I'm afraid not. I'd like to be one.'

'You just like rocks,' said Jane. She smiled again.

I wanted to say, but didn't, that I liked their precision and their purity. In those days toughness, too, was something I admired. And one of the things I liked about Jane was her tough, straightforward manner.

'That's it,' I said, 'I like rocks.'

Somehow or other we ended up in a pub in Kensington. But I don't recall that we discussed geology.

I'd drifted away from the story, thinking about Jane. The children waited, with the patience of the dispossessed, and then Tom said:

'Is that the end?'

'No, no,' I said, accelerating, 'I'm sorry. I was thinking about Mum.'

'Go on with the story could you?' said Tom.

'Sure,' I said.

'As soon as he got home, the black magician drew all the curtains, put up a sign on the door that read GONE AWAY ON BUSINESS and placed the pebble on his work-table, in a position similar to the one in which he had seen it at his brother's house.

He cleared away his work-in-progress – a formula designed to weaken the structure of heavily used bridges: he was not entirely without ambition – and began to imitate the actions of his brother. He raised his arms, shook his hands and backed away to the far wall, pressing himself into it, then carefully composed his face into fear, horror and finally a radiant smile. His plan was, when he had got the sequence of actions right, to try every single known magic word.

He could not, however, master the radiant smile at first. However hard he tried, and he practised in front of his bathroom mirror for hours, he ended up looking like someone having a tomato squashed into his face. But after a few hours and a few harsh words, the black magician managed quite a creditably radiant smile and he went back to the pebble, raised his arms, shook his hands, retreated, looked horrified, smiled, leaned over and whispered—

"Bickerton!"

You didn't know that was a magic word, did you? Well, it is. It is often used by black magicians to create feelings of gloom and despondency and I advise you never to use it if anyone you like is anywhere near you.

But, even though his every action precisely mirrored that of his brother the pebble remained just a pebble. He ran through every single word in the black magician's handbook. It did not move. He said "Hey Presto!" and "Heejus Hojus" and even the most terrible word any black magician can ever say to anything, which sounds something like "Snicklears". The pebble was still nothing more than a small grey silent object, perfectly round, perfectly composed, seeming to mock his very question by its stillness, there on the table in the dark, foul-smelling room in which he worked.

"Maybe," he said to himself, "I need to open the curtains. Perhaps this pebble only responds to white magic."

The black magician had always taken the view that there was nothing wrong with white magic *as such*. Sometimes – in the spell for creating scrofula in one-parent families, for example, or in the potion-formula for causing ambulance-drivers to lose their sense of direction, a black magician will use a certain amount of white magic in order to create an initially favourable impression with the powers of light, who take a dim view of the above-mentioned sorceries. He always maintained that *any kind of magic is fine so long as it works for you*, and, accordingly, he began to draw back the curtains, whistling to himself, in case the powers of light were looking in with his brother's interests in mind.

'Wotth the thcwofula?' said Paul.

23

'A kind of spotty disease,' I said.

'And a one parent family,' said Tom, 'is when you have just a mother.'

'Or a father,' I said.

'Yeth,' said Paul, a little nervously, I thought.

'He was extremely bad if he did that to ambulance drivers,' said Tom.

'He was,' I said, 'he was a utterly horrible person. But he was trying to sound nice. Shall I go on about him?'

'Yeth,' said Paul.

I continued.

"Oh my gosh!" he said, looking out at the road, where two or three customers were already hanging around, scuffing their shoes on the road and not daring to look at each other. "Oh my gosh! What a day!"

He sounded, I am afraid to say, very nearly sincere.

One of his customers was a lawyer who wished to put a curse on a colleague's eldest son, who was more intelligent than his own child. The black magician, squeezing his hands together, asked him to think of the blessings already bestowed on his own child. "He might not," said the black magician, "be particularly *bright* . . ."

"He's not," said the lawyer. "He's completely stupid."

"But he may have some other redeeming quality," simpered the black magician.

The lawyer was unable to think of any such quality in his son, but was so appalled by the ingratiating expression on the black magician's face that he did not pursue the matter.

Those behind the lawyer in the queue, alarmed, as we all are, by untypical behaviour, fled back down the road to report that the black magician was planning something unspeakable and that everyone had better go to bed until it was all over. The lawyer, too, went away shaking his head.

"Now," said the black magician, in a light, false tone of voice, "shall we start again?"

But it was still no use. For all he simpered and leered and grinned, the pebble remained a pebble, and though he shook his hands until they ached and smiled until he thought his face would split it refused to spin or hum or glow. The black magician became angry, and shouted out: "Tell me, you stupid pebble! Stop lying there and tell me or I'll make it very, very unpleasant for you. Spin, can't you? Hum. Or glow. Or do whatever it is you do!"

And, to his astonishment, the small grey object flickered into life. Something changed on its surface, only for a moment, so that *25* it seemed as if it would hum or spin or glow or somehow recapture that mysterious moment of change he had seen at the house of the white magician. Then the light, or movement, or sound (he could not be sure which of these it was) faded, and the pebble was once more itself – a solid, circular thing, lying in the middle of the table.

Breathlessly, the black magician approached it and put out a hand to touch it.

It was warm, as if someone had been holding it.

"Sometimes," said the black magician to himself, "it's no good asking things nicely. Sometimes you just have to show them who's boss."

He had had a lot of trouble with his bed lately which was supposed to make itself. It had got lazy, and taken to tucking in only one side of its sheet, at which the black magician had screamed at it for half an hour and threatened to take its casters off. The white magician was famous for allowing himself to be dictated to by the objects in his house, and could never ask the wardrobe to close itself without a long discussion as to whether it felt *better* with the door open.

"Clearly," said the black magician, "this is an extremely clever pebble. But it has been over-indulged."

And, after ticking it off severely (he had lost all embarrassment at the thought of talking to a pebble) he locked it in a dark desk drawer, with a particularly smelly piece of cheese.'

FIVE

'Did the white magician,' said Tom, my eldest (we were by now on the south side of the Embankment, near Vauxhall Bridge), 'find out that his pebble had been stolen?'

'Yes,' I said.

Sam, the five-year-old, pushed his huge head forward, close to the back of the driving seat. He spoke as if anxious that his question should not be overheard by the other two.

'Was he cross?' he said.

'He was very upset.'

'Did he bash him?' Sam continued.

'No,' I said. 'He didn't believe in bashing people.'

This silenced them for a moment. *What kind of a magician does this guy think he is?* I could see them thinking.

'What did he do?' asked Tom.

'He catht a thpell,' said Paul.

'No,' I said. 'He didn't.'

That brought us to a standstill.

Storytelling, of course, is as much about withholding information as imparting it. If the storyteller is to have any power at all he must retain control of his material. Easier to do, paradoxically, when dealing with witches and fairies or black and white magicians, but possible, I tell myself, even when recounting one's own small, domestic history. After all, if we can't see what's happening directly in front of us, how can we trust our own vision at all? Or our ability to transcribe that vision and make it clear to others?

'Where is Mummy?' said Sam, as I didn't seem to be continuing.

'Oh,' I said, 'she was a bit tired and felt like going home on her own. I think she fancied a change.'

The three of them looked at me with varying degrees of scepticism. It was Tom who decided to endorse this line vigorously.

'Yeah,' he said, 'she probably got bored with sitting in the *car* and fancied a tube or a bus or God knows what probably.'

'Absolutely,' I said.

'After all,' said Tom, 'a car is pretty boring. Maybe she did after all decide to go by river. By boat or hovercraft or steamer, my God who knows?'

Paul turned his large, blonde head towards his elder brother.

'*If*,' he said, 'she wath going by boat or hovercraft, or *thteamer*, Why didn't she take uth with her?'

This silenced everyone. Sam looked suddenly panic-stricken.

'Why?' he said, his mouth turning down.

Everyone looked at me. 'Because,' I said, 'you can't take the car on the boat. Or the hovercraft.'

'You can,' said Paul, 'from Dover.'

'We are not *in* Dover,' I said.

The difficult subject of the whereabouts of their mother seemed to have been dealt with. There are some parents, I suppose, who would propose that children should be told the truth at all times – and that the stories we tell them, whether they are concerned with how babies arrive or why so and so swept out of the house that morning, had better, for all our sakes, be honest from the word go.

SIX

The fact of the matter is, however, that children, like adults, listen to what they want to hear. There are only certain stories that satisfy them, and those are the ones that we had better learn to tell. Family life cannot afford to be an endless quest for truth and honesty. In the quiet order of my parent's house no one enquired too closely when my father disappeared for the occasional weekend away. Marriage is, as far as I can see, very often a matter of each partner getting their story straight.

'Where wath the magician?' said Paul.

'Sorry?' I said.

'What country wath he in?'

I looked out at the river. We were nearly home.

'Oh', I said, 'just a country. With roads and trees and houses. And a king.'

They were quiet again. Attentive.

'Yes, yes, yes', I went on. 'In the country where all this happened there was a king and the king had ministers, and it wasn't very long before the king got to hear about the magic pebble.

The king had about two hundred highly qualified black magicians at court (he kept two white magicians for state occasions) and they made it their business to find out what every other black magician in the country was doing.

Which was why the black magicians, in talking about their work, were always extremely cautious. When they met each other at conferences, or at the kind of social gatherings they liked, the average black magician would say, if asked what he was doing:

"Oh, nothing much. This and that. This and that."

While, all the time, he was working some enviable new way of making life miserable.

Any advance in black magic, any new curse or spell was always a jealously guarded secret; even after its inventor had perfected, say, a formula for ensuring bad weather on national holidays, he or she would wait for years before deciding to whom they could trust it. Sometimes they kept their discoveries a secret for so long they forgot them entirely.

But, of course, they all talked behind each other's backs, and it wasn't long before the king heard that a black magician in a distant part of the country had a pebble that could give off heat and light and noise. It could sing, too, some of the court black magicians said; it could make delicious meals appear from nowhere and maim or kill anyone within a thirty-yards radius.

The king was extremely excited.

Before he had even seen it he made a long speech about the pebble, saying what an enormous benefit it was going to be for mankind. "We are on the threshold," he said, "of a time when man will be able to explore more of the deepest secrets of the world than ever before." He commanded that the pebble be brought to him at once.

The pebble, and the black magician, duly appeared. But although the black magician bowed over it, waved his hands, whispered and cajoled, the pebble remained nothing more than a pebble. The more he carried on (by the end he was screaming and

30

shouting at it and telling it to behave with more respect in front of the royal family) the more simply pebbly it seemed to become. It was, by the time he had finished, almost triumphantly, defiantly pebble-like. People agreed they had never seen anything quite so solid and grey and stony, anything less likely to hum or spin or rotate.

"My brother could do it," muttered the black magician as, amid the jeers of the courtiers, he prepared to put the pebble back into the box.

"Then bring him here," said the king. "*Now.*"

Messengers were sent to bring the white magician. When he arrived, everyone was highly amused at the sight of him. He wore a conical white hat, a white robe with a large W on it and a huge red scarf which he wound round his neck like a tame snake. His shoes, everyone agreed, were quite ridiculously long. His face was round and fat and jolly and everyone at court who cared about Style and Fashion found him ridiculous. All courtiers were taught to cultivate what was called "the court expression" – which meant focusing both eyes on the tip of one's nose, turning both corners of the mouth down, and walking as if someone had lodged a truncheon up one's behind. In fact, as the white magician was brought through to the king people openly pointed and laughed at him and said loudly to each other that he obviously lacked drive or charisma or any of the other things prized at court. But the expression on the magician's face did not alter, and when he was face to face with the king he did not bow but looked him straight in the eyes, since old white magicians say *all men are my brothers and I kneel to none.*

He didn't look at all surprised at seeing his pebble again. In fact he didn't look at it as if it were "his" at all.

The pebble lay on a velvet cushion just next to the throne, guarded by three crack soldiers of the King's Own Hussars.

"I hear', said the king, "that you can do things with this pebble.   *31*

I hear it hums and spins and rotates and—"

"Tells the time," said a black magician, "and detects forged money and—"

The king held up his hand. He screwed himself down into his throne and cocked his crown at a rakish angle. He was known as a king who was good with people, and he prided himself on being able to talk to the ordinary man, even when he was as freakish as this one.

"Come on," he said. "Do us a favour, son. Eh?"

The white magician looked at the king long and hard. Then he

looked over at his brother who was fidgeting from one foot to the other, just behind the cushion on which the pebble lay.

"I only wish I could," he said. "If only it were as simple as that. But I am afraid it isn't."

"No?" said the king, rather meanly.

"No," said the white magician. "And if I were you I would not meddle in this matter any longer. For there is a great and terrible secret here, which I wish I was not burdened with."

The king leaned forward.

"Are you saying," he said, in a cold voice, "that you won't get this pebble to do whatever it does?"

There was a very long pause.

"Yes," said the white magician. "I suppose I am."

And *then—*'

SEVEN

Well, then we arrived home.

Jane wasn't there, but the children didn't seem to notice. They were much more interested, at first anyway, in what the king did next.

Perhaps I told the story better then; I don't know. I certainly wouldn't have used some of the words I have used here. I am sure there were far more jokes about lavatories in it. I think my black magician's words were calculated to amuse the children. I think the worst thing a black magician could say was 'Wogan' or 'bottom'. In telling the story now I used the name of a perfectly inoffensive little man at my office. I don't know why.

I'm retelling the story now, and changing it as I tell it, because, for some reason, I want it to last. I want other people to hear the story. I want the private act to become a little more public. Why? Because I suppose I want to preserve that moment, and so many other moments in that curious Spring. I want you to understand how, well, how *beautiful* it was, to drive along that afternoon, through London, and catch their faces in the driving mirror, white and attentive.

I'm sorry to have to use the word 'beautiful'. These days it isn't a word I like much. It seems to me as suspect and imprecise as the word 'racist' or 'sexist'. I have broken off retelling my story to look at a newspaper picture of the British Labour leader, Neil Kinnock, who is sitting next to President Reagan in the White House. I mention it because it is the sort of thing adults like to hear about. Isn't it? Kinnock is gesturing wildly yet amicably, his lower lip thrust out. He looks absorbed in his own eloquence and, at the same time, curiously trustful of it, as if he hopes its charm and obvious sincerity are going to make the American President like him. Hopes. He doesn't look entirely sure this will happen.

President Reagan looks as if someone has just shot him in the back, but he's putting a brave face on it. He is focusing, without apparent enthusiasm, on a spot on the floor, about ten yards in front of him. At any moment, I think, looking at this photograph of the President, sawdust is about to start leaking from his head.

They are talking, according to the newspaper in which this picture appears, about nuclear weapons. Neil Kinnock is telling President Reagan that the British people don't want American nuclear weapons over in Britain. Or, at least, he's sort of saying that. He's saying that this is the sort of thing he may well end up thinking if things go on the way they're going. And President Reagan is nodding and smiling as if he knows something Neil Kinnock doesn't.

Actually the paper has probably got it wrong. They're probably talking about the merits of Club Class on Pan Am flights out of Kennedy. Kinnock is probably demonstrating his badminton stroke. It doesn't really matter what they're saying about nuclear weapons, because whatever either of them say nuclear weapons are *there*, in silos, submarines, on blasted heaths, locked in enchanted castles, lovingly tended by bad magicians. They are waiting, all the way from Nevada to Norwich, waiting like a pike in the rocks, blue and khaki, steel and rubber, waiting for the moment when a hand reaches out and—

I told the children I would continue the story another day. *35*

They went upstairs to watch a serial on the television. In this episode, three American policemen shot some robbers. I sat downstairs and waited for Jane.

She didn't come.

She didn't come when I made their tea. She didn't come when Sam cried because Paul had taken his pencil. She didn't come when I got their pyjamas on and brushed their teeth and told them what she usually tells them – that it was late and they would be tired and their homework would suffer. I performed all these necessary tasks with the intensity of one who repeats a magical charm. *If I do this*, I kept thinking, *she'll arrive back.*

But she didn't come. She didn't come when, near desperation, I sent them up to watch television again and began to telephone our friends.

As I telephoned I realised, with some horror, that we had started to have different friends. This wasn't always the case. Once, years ago, people had said they couldn't tell us apart, and we refused to separate our opinion of mutual acquaintances. We agreed about them in the way we agreed about the Labour Party or the best place to choose for a holiday.

Back then we agreed about the Bomb. I think we both agreed it was a Bad Idea. And, once we had thought that, neither of us thought there was any need to think any more about it. And now, it seemed, the Bomb was dividing us, making us think in different ways. Perhaps, I thought wildly, it's operating on us like a virus, fogging our moral perceptions so that it can assert itself when its time comes.

None of our friends had seen her. I went in to see the children and found them watching a video of the story they had been watching earlier. The same three American policemen pushed the same robbers down the same spiral staircase. The robbers fell in the same heap and the same section of the wall fell in on them, spattering them with dust and provoking the same comic cough from the fattest of the villains. The children, when they saw this, gave the same laugh; my eldest son fell back and slapped his thigh in the same slightly artificial way, while Paul lay on his stomach, in the same position on the floor, one leg cocked up behind him like some curious predatory marsh bird. Sam crossed the same small, chubby legs in the same manner. None of them turned to look at me.

'Shall I go on with my story?' I said.

They didn't answer. Eventually Paul said, 'Sure', but he did not take his eyes off the television screen.

Then I heard the front door open and Jane's familiar step in the hall. I went to the landing and looked down.

What I couldn't understand was that her hair, her beautiful, long blonde hair, was soaking wet. It hadn't been raining. At first I thought she must have walked through a thunderstorm. Then I saw that her coat and face weren't wet. Just her hair. I let her hang up her coat and walk through to the kitchen, and waited for the sounds of cupboard doors being opened and biscuits being crunched.

She needs to re-possess the house first, I thought. *I'll wait.*

I went downstairs. She was kneeling by the fridge and, when she looked up, there was no change of expression in her eyes.

'Hi!' I said.

'Hullo.'

She said this as if she was trying to think about what the greeting meant while she said it. When she had finished saying it she paused, as if its newly discovered purpose did not please her. Then she went back to the fridge. *She's been acting strangely of late*, I thought. *Is she all right?*

'What's up?' I said.

She shrugged. 'Nothing.'

I went over to her. He hair was matted together, streaked darkly with water. *Has she been in someone's house?* I thought.   *37*

Making love with someone? Then showered?

The guilty, the unfaithful, suspect others of their own mis-deeds. But because they do not wish to be hurt they assume their partner's betrayal of them to be of an entirely different order than their own – wicked in quite another way.

Perhaps, I thought, she's having it off with a teacher, probably called Kevin. Perhaps they go to bed together and discuss how to stamp out racism and sexism and nuclear bombs and he climaxes to an image of the end of Britain as a colonial power. Or else (I was beginning to enjoy the idea of her being unfaithful) in the act of love they use the words that are most racist, most sexist, most nuclear, most forbidden. 'Give it to me hard with your big Cruise Missile' she moans, while Kevin, all thought of ILEA and the need to fight for grass-roots democracy in the Labour Party forgotten, bares his teeth and screams appalling things about negroes.

I looked at her. She seemed, suddenly, very small and old and insecure. I had a sudden powerful sense that her wet hair was to do with some awful, private misery of hers and that I must be patient and wait to find out what it was. I remembered how I checked my back for scratch marks after being with my soprano and suddenly *I* felt guilty. She wasn't hiding her hair. She turned her head to me as if she wanted me to comment on it and, as she did this, I found I could not. I went to her and put my arms round her, but she still didn't move.

'Look,' I said, 'let's go away together. With the children.'
'Okay,' she said.

Only then did she relax her shoulders and allow me to hold her the way I used to, before the children were born and took our innocence from us.

'Let's go up the Thames Valley,' she said.

EIGHT

We have both lived our lives on, or near, the Thames.

Jane was born in Oxford and I in South-East London, and, since our separate childhoods in the 1950s, we've seen it change. Up near where Jane was born the river is now crowded with boats, but from Deptford to Tilbury, these days, the grey current shoulders on towards the sea, uncluttered.

We spent that holiday on a barge, starting from Pangbourne, thirty or so miles West of London, where the river has started to twist, almost desperately, towards Oxford, fooling away the traveller's sense of time and place. When we started towards Oxford, and Jane's parents' home, I thought I knew which market towns lay ahead. Henley, wasn't it? Or Marlow? Wallingford? But, as we glided upstream – Paul lying on the prow, one leg cocked up behind him, staring into the green and silver river – I lost all sense of East and West. I felt I was climbing some elaborate stairway, devised in an Escher drawing, the only thing pulling me forward being the gentle flow of the Thames against us, and the curiously tough words used in the soft navigation of a stream – *up* river, towards the *higher* reaches, *high, high up towards the source.*

Jane sat on the roof of the barge and, like her middle son, she stared into the water. She didn't say much.

On the second day I started the story again. It was Paul who persuaded me. I didn't like the idea of Jane listening, but after a while I almost forgot she was there. And I couldn't bear not to satisfy his simple hunger to know. 'What', he kept saying, 'did the king do to the white magician to get him to make the magic pebble do itth thtuff?' 'He tortured him,' said my eldest son, looking up from *The Dragon of Despair: Test Your Skill Against the Witch of Blacklock Castle.*

'You're right,' I said. 'He tortured him most horribly.'

'How?' said Paul. 'How did he torture him? Did he thtrap him to a crocodile?'

'If you want to know,' I said, 'I'll tell you. The king tortured the white magician in several different ways, but the worst of these was undoubtedly the torture of the biscuits.'

'The *what?*'

'Have you never heard of the torture of the biscuits?'

'Good torture,' said Paul.

'Have you never heard of the torture of the biscuits? It sounds almost pleasant, doesn't it? But it is in fact a loathsome and horrible torture, so horrible that even the Witch of Blacklock Castle has been known to abjure her odious witcheries under it. And, as I am sure you know, the Witch of Blacklock Castle has been known to cut slices off men *while they are still alive* and serve their own flesh to them wrapped up like a Doner Kebab.

The torture of the biscuits works like this.

The victim is taken to a small, comfortable room and sat in an easy chair. He is given biscuits. *Ah ha*, he thinks. *Call this torture?* There are chocolate creams and digestives, Garibaldis and Butterthins, there are petits fours and cheese biscuits, marshmallows and hundreds of varieties of shortbread. There are the more vulgar kinds of biscuit too. Twix Bars and Club bars and things called Shout and Jump and Twist. There are Wagonwheels and elaborately wrapped chocolate bars that have probably lain for years in the research and development department of major confectioners, waiting for just this moment. Things with names like Beast and Cor and Whoopsee and an extraordinary biscuit from Japan, moulded in a curious shape and filled with marzipan and called Bum biscuit.

'Right,' says the torturer. 'Eat!'

And the victim eats.

At first the biscuits taste pleasant enough. But then, when the empty tin is replaced with another, identical selection, they begin to taste sour and stale. The victim chews more and more slowly, and the crumbs gum up his mouth. Then, when the second tin is empty, more biscuits are brought and his torturers stand over him and make it clear that he must eat. They taste like sawdust now. He can hardly move his jaws. He protests, but one torturer holds him while the other forces the biscuits past his protesting tongue, gagging him. They soak the biscuits in water, to soften them, to make it easier to force them into his mouth. They push him to the floor, and, though he gasps and calls for mercy, they do not stop.

Just when he thinks he can take no more, that he will die, they stop and leave him alone for two days. When he is once again able to talk normally, when he thinks there is some chance left for him, to lead his life as he was leading it before, another torturer comes into his cell.

With him he carries a full tin of biscuits.

That is the point at which the victim usually confesses. Some go through the process again. A few two or three times. Some brave men go through it four or five or six times, but in the end they always break down and confess because they realise the supply of biscuits is endless.

'Why doeth it alwayth have to be bithcuith?' said Paul.

'It doesn't have to be,' I said. 'I made it biscuits because you like biscuits. It can be anything. It is best if it is something you really   *41* like because the whole point of the torture is to turn something you like into something horrible, so that you are no longer certain of anything.'

I looked up at Jane. She gave no sign that she could hear what we were saying. 'You see,' I went on, 'it's good not to be certain about things. But you shouldn't be too uncertain. If you're too uncertain, about your country or about someone you love very much or about yourself it poisons you and leaves you nothing.'

'Did the white magician tell the king how to work the pebble?' said Paul, implacably.

Jane turned towards me, her long, golden hair down her back. She was studying me the way she had studied me that day we came back from Greenwich, as if seeing me for the first time.

'No,' I said, 'he was the only man in the world ever to survive the torture of the biscuits.'

When I started the story again I was more confident with it. It had been some weeks since I had talked about the characters, and they had not, until Paul's question, started to live for me. It was his stern, enquiring expression that conjured them up and, as I talked, I tried to make them as clear and sharp and simple as he seemed to me then. And, to my surprise, I forgot the children as I talked. I forgot the boat and its sway and pull against the current. I forgot my wife's pale, almost haunted expression, and told my story.

I thought about this white magician I had invented. I had given him a round face, a Father Christmas figure. But now he was suffering (and I had started to believe in his suffering) I saw him differently. He had a pale, sad face, like an El Greco figure. He had long tapering fingers and huge watchful eyes. And the knowledge he was protecting seemed suddenly real. That was why he was suffering. He was suffering, like Galileo, for the sake of learning. And, as I talked on, the boat slid upstream and the magician and his unearthly country became as real to me as the green

42

unfolding trees that lowered out across the water, filtering the Spring sun in constant moving patterns across the river as it flowed gently back towards the city.

NINE

'All that the white magician would say in reply to the questions put to him by the king's torturers was this:

"The first word you say, will make the pebble spin.

"The second word once spoken all our troubles shall begin."

The king's torturers did not understand this. Was it a code of some kind? If it wasn't a code then what did it mean? And how would it help them to make the magic pebble obey them?

Sometimes, when he was most in agony, they leaned over him and heard him muttering something. It sounded as if he were saying the same word over and over again. The word sounded like "good". But who was good? The magician? What had good, they asked themselves, to do with any of this? But, however hard they tortured him, he would never say more than:

"The first word will make the pebble hum and spin.

At the second word our troubles will end or begin."

His brother, the black magician, was held at the court under house arrest. He spent a great deal of time trying to ingratiate himself with his jailers, writing letters to persons in authority, protesting his loyalty to the king, but his spirit was broken. Out in the provinces he had never seen real evil. Here, at court, where betrayal was a way of life, the black magician's attempts at malice

44

seemed almost laughable.

Every month they took him to see his brother, who was kept in a cell a long way underground, and left him alone with the white magician in the hope that his brother might then confess the secret of the pebble. But he never did.

All the black magician's malice against his brother could not have devised the things that the king made the white magician suffer. Day by day he grew thinner and weaker; day after day he

was insulted, wounded and mistreated. But still he would not talk to his jailers. And, as the black magician sat in silence in his cell, listening to the rustle of the king's informers in the corridor, there came the beginnings of something not wholly bad in him. Not tenderness – because he didn't know how to be gentle; not compassion – because he could not imagine what it was like to be anyone apart from himself; but a kind of fear. A fear and a sense of waste.

The black magician knew that if his brother did not tell his secret the king would kill both of them.

"Look," he said, after a more than usually long silence, "just give me a clue . . .".

His brother looked at him wearily.

"There are two words," the white magician said at last. "Two words."

"I have tried every word I know," said his brother.

"It is who says the words," said the white magician.

"You mean it has to be you?"

The white magician sighed and passed a hand over his brow.

"Only a good man can know its secrets," he said. "And only a man perfect in the search for knowledge can make it obey his commands. But I must warn you—"

The black magician didn't wait for the warning. He scurried out of the cell and demanded an audience with the king. The king was delighted. They took the white magician away to a larger, cleaner cell, and the king, his ministers and magicians had a meeting.

"What this means," said the king, "is that we, or rather *you*," (here he looked rather meanly at his courtiers) "have been doing the wrong kind of magic. We don't want black magic. We want white magic. *Good* magic. That's what this pebble responds to. Because white magic, in case any of you had forgotten, means loving your neighbour and curing diseases and all of that and can

46

we have a little less of the black magic and a bit more of the white, please? Because with a bit of that we may be able to understand this magic pebble which is clearly a lot more dangerous and interesting than any of your enchantments."

The king had no evidence for supposing the pebble to be in any way remarkable. But rumour is always more powerful, to those in power, than the evidence of their senses, and anything that will not obey those accustomed to command intrigues and beckons them on.

Everyone had forgotten about white magic. They had forgotten about being good, of course, but they had totally and utterly and completely forgotten about white magic. It was difficult and dangerous and slow and badly paid and terribly hard to learn, and even when you had learned it you had probably learned it all wrong, which was why it was confined to a few solitary people the length and breadth of the kingdom. But when the king gave an order it was obeyed; people were ordered to be cheerful and helpful and kind. Anyone *not* being cheerful and helpful and kind would be locked up and tortured most horribly.

The white magician was released from prison and told he was to be given a castle, some miles to the west of the city, where he was to be allowed to found a school of white magic. He was going to be given servants and as much money as he wanted. Black magic was to be banned from every part of the kingdom.

"We want to learn," said the king, "we want to be good so that we can learn. We understand. We want to be *perfect in the search for knowledge. Right?"*

The white magician looked very serious.

"I don't know what my brother has told you," he said, "but I am sure he has not told you everything."

The king looked at the white magician suspiciously.

"What," he said slowly, "do you mean? *Everything?"*

"I will tell you," said the white magician, "the story of how I   47 came by that pebble, and how terrible is its secret and why I do not trust myself to wish to command it and what are the terms of the prophecy.''

"Prophecy?'' said the king, who felt he was getting somewhere at last. "What prophecy?''

"I will tell you,'' said the white magician, "everything. But first I must tell you the story of how I came by the pebble. Only I am very weak through long months of imprisonment, and before I tell you I must rest and be fed.''

The king told him he had already executed those responsible for the white magician's imprisonment, at which the white magician became extremely angry, and it wasn't until the king explained he was merely having a *royal joke* and that in fact his imprisonment had been caused by *clerical error* that the white magician agreed to accept food and rest, and in due course to tell the court how and where he had found the magic pebble.

He believed, you must understand, that people told the truth, and it took very little to deceive him.'

"It's not,' said my eldest son, 'always a good idea to tell the truth.'

'It is,' I said.

'Not always,' he replied, 'if you were a spy right? And someone wanted to know what the plans were you wouldn't tell them right?'

The other two looked at him with great respect.

'It would depend', I said, 'who they are.'

'That's what I mean precisely,' said my eldest.

I had no immediate answer to this. I looked down at the water. Its surface picked up the light like some discreet, expensive jewel. Below, you could see the river, thick, dark, mysterious, decorated with side-currents, fissures, ridges endlessly multiplying and collapsing formations.

48   'The rule,' I said 'is to tell the truth wherever possible.'

He looked at me shrewdly. I looked away. Jane was staring at the bank. She looked as if she was waiting for someone to take a photograph of her. To avoid further discussion about truth-telling, I returned to my story.

'After he had eaten and rested,' I said, 'he was dressed in splendid white robes and brought into the Great Hall. The king motioned all to be silent and the white magician began. And the faces of the court, the magicians, the ministers, the ladies-in-waiting, the great lords of the army, all were as absorbed and attentive as children, listening to a story from their father, driving home from some excursion, his voice as steady and powerful as an enchantment.'

TEN

' "I was born near a river.

"It was a clear, beautiful river and it flowed from my house, through level fields and woods, to a great city on a plain. And from the plain it flowed to the sea, where great ships carried corn and wood and precious jewels to all parts of the world.

"Where I was born the river was young, and clear. Every day I went down to the river and played. I splashed and swam. I watched the herons beat out from the trees or lumber up into the air from their fishing pitches, and I listened to the clear murmur of the water as it washed over the pebbles that lay on the bed of the stream.

"They were so clean, those pebbles! So untouched! Further down the river was driftwood and oil and the wreckage and waste that people had brought, but up here, where I was born, everything was fresh.

"And there was one pebble, at the bottom of the deepest, clearest pool, that seemed shinier than all the others. But, however many times I swam down to it, I could never bring it to the surface. I would hold my breath and scrabble along the bottom of the pool, and often would break the surface of the river, convinced that I held the pebble in my hands. But when I looked I always saw that, though what I had was shining and perfect, the most perfect and bright pebble was still there, where it had always been, out of reach but clearly to be seen through the water.

"It was, I felt sure, a magic pebble.

"I was young, but I knew enough to realise that, if I were patient, and sat alone on the bank of that river, I would learn more. I would not be able to grasp the pebble for myself, but someone, or something, would come to the river one night or morning to gaze at its treasure. For someone or something was guarding it, of that I was certain, and with a magic stronger than any I knew.

"I hid in the bushes, a little way from the river, and I watched.

"For days nothing happened. The sheep were higher up on the cropped grass (we were close to the lower slopes of a great mountain where I was born), on the heath above us the lapwings cried, but no one – apart from, once, a shepherd – came to the pool where the magic pebble lay.

"And then, one day, a beautiful girl came down through the rocks and the cropped grass and she stood at the edge of the pool.

"She wasn't one of the village girls. I had never seen her before. She had long blonde hair that fell down her back and she carried a book with her, a heavy book, bound in brown velvet and tied with a huge, bronze clasp. She looked graceful and calm and wise. She was wearing a loose dress, printed with flowers of all different colours and sizes and on her feet she wore a pair of brown sandals.

"She knelt down by the side of the river and took off her dress. She had beautiful white skin and shoulders as smooth as pumice stone, but I was ashamed to look at her. As I watched she leaned forward and her right hand seemed to grow, endlessly, like some monstrous plant. It arched forward into the water and when it broke the surface I saw, cupped in her white palm, was the pebble. She placed the pebble on the side of the pool.

"Then she leaned over the water, lowered her head and *51*

allowed her beautiful hair to trail in the water. When it was all bound together, in a dripping sheet, she caught it up with her two hands and shook it out. Then she lowered it once more into the river and pulled it back again. This time she spread it out to dry behind her, all down her naked back, and kneeling as if in prayer, she showed her hair to the sun, while I looked on, my mouth dry with fear and shame, for I had seen what I knew I should not have seen.

"I don't know how she heard me. Perhaps I moved. But suddenly she turned towards the bushes, and I knew she had seen my face. Our eyes met and, as they met, she began to change.

"Her white skin grew scales, like a fish's scales. Her hands buckled up as if in the grip of some terrible arthritis, and when the joints had swollen to a grotesque size I saw they were encrusted with thick, yellow skin, as you see on a chicken's feet. Her straight white back bowed and curved hideously, and her waist and legs puckered up into her belly, until it was hard to tell whether she went on two or four legs or no legs at all.

"But it was her eyes that frightened me most. Through all these changes her eyes had seemed to stay the same, and there was a note of pleading in them, as if there were some gentle human soul that knew itself to be trapped in this hideous body. And then, as I watched, the eyes changed. The pupils narrowed to a point and the iris and the whites began to melt into each other. As the blue of one and the creamy porcelain of the other mixed, they darkened until the whole eye, save for the pupil, was black. But in the middle of the black, like an angry pin-prick, was a red, evil, fiery glow.

"Do you want my pebble?' said the thing – I could not longer call it a woman – in a wheedling, mocking tone.

"I did not answer. It shuffled towards me and put its head to one side.

"'Imagine', said the thing, 'being able to make the world obey

you. To make trees bow down and stones to speak.'

"Its thin, insidious voice seemed to be coming, not from the creature's mouth, but from inside my head.

"'Imagine making trees wither and stones to break apart. Imagine, the world as your servant. Imagine.'

"It was close enough to touch me now.

"'There are two charms that must be spoken', said the thing, 'and the first must be spoken by a good man and the second must be spoken by a man perfect in the search for knowledge. At the speaking of the first charm, the pebble will show its power. And then—'

"And then what?'

"I stepped towards it but my legs felt heavy. I did not appear to be moving and could no longer tell whether its voice was outside or inside my head.

"*The first word you say will make the pebble spin.*

At the second word spoken our troubles shall begin'.

"I wanted to ask it what those words meant, and what the two charms that might give me power over the pebble might be. But the thing had started to laugh, a horrible, brass, empty laugh. As it did so it rocked from side to side, and as it rocked I seemed to see through it the image it had first taken – the form of a beautiful woman. And was *this* its true nature? I wondered. Was it condemned to this hideous shape? For the beautiful woman's long blonde hair lay down her back, still wet from the river. And she was crying, as if she saw things too painful and horrible for my imagination.

"Then there was no one but myself and the river and the uncluttered sky.

"I clambered out of the bushes and walked down to the edge of the pool. I could see the pebble, on the bottom, where it had always been, clear, distinct. I dived in, swam down to it and reached towards where I thought it lay.

"The blood hummed in my ears as I groped for the stone, but as soon as I had it in my grasp I was sure that this time I had not been deceived. Once back on the riverbank, the pebble in my hand, I looked back into the pool, but I could not see any stone brighter or clearer than the rest: what I held in my hands was the stone I wanted.

"And, when I realised this was the case, I found I knew the two words that must be spoken to make the pebble obey me. But I knew also the meaning of the rhyme. The first word must be spoken by a good man, and then the pebble would show its power. But the second word must be spoken by a man perfect in the search for knowledge. And if the word is spoken by one *not* perfect in this way, then will our troubles begin.

"It was for this that I took up the study of white magic and studied as hard as I was able. And when I had the temerity to think I was indeed a good man I spoke the first word I had been given, at which, indeed, that pebble glowed or changed or spun, I could not say, but it showed promise of such power and strangeness that even now I dare not think of it. But how can I tell you the second word, knowing as I do the terms of the prophecy? For all around me, even my brother who first told you of all of this, study very different things. And how can we find a man perfect in the search for knowledge when all we study is vice and meanness, pettiness, greed and spite? For I tell you I am sure that what I saw in that girl's face will come to pass if the second word is spoken by one *not perfect in the search for knowledge.*"

At this point the king looked sternly round at his courtiers.

"You hear him," he said, "you know what he means?"

They all looked very ashamed and nervous. The king went over to the white magician and took his right hand between his two palms.

"Now," said the white magician, "perhaps you understand why I did not wish the pebble to fall into the wrong hands."

"My God now," said a courtier. "Suppose some foreigner got hold of it!"

The king looked into the white magician's eyes and he sounded very honest and sincere, as he said: "We will all work hard to be good. We will all study and work and try to be worthy of this great gift. And one day I hope we will be ready to pronounce this second great word of which you have told us. If we are worthy it may mean the end, not the beginning of all our troubles."

Everyone agreed that this was a brave and eloquent speech. The courtiers applauded violently and threw their caps, if they were wearing them, into the air. One very senior black magician 55 took off his hat, threw it to the ground and stamped on it, saying he could scarcely bear to look at something so evil. Only the white magician continued to stare at the king. He alone of all the company did not applaud.

"It is very hard to be good," he said, when the applause had died away. "You have to practise, practise, practise. . . . But to be perfect? In the search for knowledge?"

And he gave a small, despairing shrug, and his big lemur's eyes looked sorrowful.

So it happened that everyone in the kingdom, from the poorest peasant to the most important members of the royal family, was told to be good. And, indeed, they did try to be good. The pebble was kept under lock and key at the newly founded School of White Magic, while all waited for the time when a man could be found who was perfect in the search for knowledge, who was both wise and good enough to speak the second charm.'

ELEVEN

'Why,' said Paul, 'couldn't the white magician thpeak the charm? If he wath good. If he wath perfect in the thearch for knowledge.'

'Because,' I said, steering the boat towards the bank, 'kingdoms are never run by magicians.'

'That's true actually, Paul,' said his eldest brother. 'Magicians sort of *work for* kings. Kings make the decisions.'

Paul was not to be deflected. 'If,' he said, 'the white magician had the pebble, couldn't he thort of *blatht* anyone who argued with him. Including the King?'

'That wouldn't be good, though, would it?' I said. 'You had to be good to use this pebble, remember.'

Sam looked up at me wildly. Like many five-year-olds, he spent his life in a waking dream, touching down occasionally in a time zone of his own.

'Did you', he said, 'have to go to bed early to use this pebble?'

'You did,' I said. 'And you had to brush your teeth and practise your recorder and be very polite to grown-ups.'

'And den,' said Sam, lapsing rather self-consciously into baby talk, 'you could smash anyone wiv der pebble.'

'I don't think', said Jane, 'that your attempts at moral instruction through the medium of narrative, are quite working.'

We were almost at the bank. The Spring sun was fading. Ahead of us was a quiet field that faced another quiet field, fringed by trees. There were no roads or houses or PRIVATE signs to be seen. It was simply a piece of England in which no one but us, for the moment, seemed to have an interest.

'Shall we moor here?' I said.

'If you like,' said Jane.

As we tied up the boat, Jane and I discussed the moral implications of narrative. Could stories tell people how to lead better lives? Should anyone try to tell anyone else how to lead a better life? How did one lead a better life anyway? Was it possible? What were we doing here, in the Thames valley, while Amal militiamen shot women in the Lebanon, while nuclear warheads slumbered miles to the East of us?

Once we were on to nuclear warheads, the conversation became less amicable.

'We have to stop talking,' said Jane, 'and *do* something.'

She didn't like my story, she said. She wanted to know why, as usual in fairy tales, it was all the woman's fault. Did women invent nuclear weapons? she asked me. I said the story wasn't necessarily about nuclear weapons. She said the worst thing about it was that it so obviously was. It was a dumb allegory, she said. The pebble was the bomb, right? An invention that would make or mar mankind? Right? The white magician was obviously Oppenheimer and the king was the postwar American government. For 'be good' read 'fight for democracy', right? Why had I made Einstein a woman – and a monstrous, witch-like woman into the bargain? Was this some slur on Marie Curie? And, while we were at it, if I was going to give the children allegory, I might at least check my facts. What about Rutherford's structure for the atom? And, while we were at it, how was I going to develop this rather crude little fable? Presumably they were all going to become virtuous, and use the pebble as a major energy source? Was this the idea? I should sell the fucking story,' said she, 'to the Atomic Energy Authority. They should mount a production of it at Sellafield, along with that stupid fucking advert that is supposed to tell everyone how safe and clean and good nuclear power is and how the rivers and streams are pure and fresh and sweet and will stay so as long as we stay away from women with long blonde hair and ideas above their station. Crazy women who guard the rivers where they grew up, who haunt them and—

'You're not crazy,' I said.

The children were off, deep into the field by now, gathering sticks. Sam was standing on his own in his red football shorts. His concentration gave him an air of sadness.

'That day at Greenwich,' I said. 'Did you—'

'Did I what?'

'I don't know,' I said. 'I had this crazy idea. That you went down to the river. And went down the steps, there, below Greenwich. And looked at the current for a long time. And then leaned slowly forward and dipped your hair in the stream. In the river.'

She put her hair to one side. When she spoke her voice had a strained, nervous quality to it.

'Pretty filthy river,' she said.

She laughed, high-pitched, nervous.

'You could have done anything that day,' I said.

'Well, I am crazy,' she said. 'Aren't I? I'm a crazy woman. One of those crazy women you see about the place who dance on the top of silos and doesn't see the need for fine moral arguments but want something *done*, even if it's only a gesture. Can't a gesture means something? Like those women at the Pentagon who put flowers in the gun barrels of the soldiers? Remember that? Maybe all women should do that. Go down to the river and wash their hair in it and say to the men and the soldiers, "There – you cannot step into the same river twice but if you go on robbing and stealing and spoiling the river the way you have been you will be able to step into it as many times as you want because it will

59

always be the same river, always dead, polluted, dangerous."'

She stopped, her face flushed. I had seen her look like that once, years ago, when she was ill. She had had a breakdown at her parents' place, not so far from here, and, one night, she had gone down to the river, alone, and sat by it for hours. A neighbour had seen her, fortunately. As he watched, from the other side of the river where we moored the boat, Jane had fallen forwards into the water, like Ophelia, and floated face-down, her hair spread out around her in the current, like some exotic water plant. I can't remember how he got her out but somehow he did.

I saw her later, in the hospital, and she had that look.

'Christ,' she said, 'you do think I'm barmy, don't you?'

'No,' I said, 'I don't.'

She pushed her face into mine. 'Well,' she said. 'Try and act as if you don't think I'm barmy.'

Then she grinned. 'What a nice idea,' she said, 'washing your hair in the river. To see if it'll come clean.'

The river *or* the hair? *Washed my hands in muddy water, washed my hands in the muddy stream. Tried to do all the things I oughter. But I must have washed my hands in the muddy stream.*

It was curious.

I hadn't wanted her to hear the story. I had wanted it to be something shared between me and my sons. Since I had left them to her for so long I wanted a secret that was ours. What better secret than a story? Women, I thought bitterly, share their secrets openly in front of males, glorying in their untouchable privacy, a privacy that can survive the most flagrantly exhibited scrutiny. I recalled standing next to Jane and her friends in the school playground, listening to their talk while at the same time being barred from it by a delicacy that was, to me, as threatening and impregnable as that wire perimeter fence at Greenham Common.

'You', her friend would say, '*are* your weight. You're happy in your body. Now my hips and *thighs* . . .'

We the males are like my five-year-old son, still wrapped in our childhood stories and adventures, that are never, unlike girl's stories, about the real world. We are still touching down on a planet we have totally failed to understand, that, for all we know of it, might as well be peopled by dragons and black magicians and pebbles that glow and spin and hum and threaten to make or mar.

It was that evening that Jane started to refuse food.

We were eating very simply. I had opened two tins of beans and some bacon. Jane said she wasn't hungry. That didn't surprise me. The moment when I saw that this was the beginning of something more important, the kind of gesture she had spoken of earlier that evening, was when Paul offered her the biscuit tin. His small, compact face, framed by blonde hair, was all solicitude.

'Have a bithcuit', he said.

Jane put out her hand and touched his cheek.

'No thanks, love', she said.

'Pleath', said Paul.

He sounded worried. It didn't seem right that she shouldn't eat. She was being curiously distant with him.

'No thanks, love', she said again.

'Jutht one', pleaded Paul.

She would have given in to him then, normally. She might not have eaten all the biscuit, nibbling a little then concealing it or at least promising to eat it later but, like the good girl she always was, cleaning her plate for Mummy and Daddy, and now for son and heir. But she didn't. She would not take the biscuit.

'Ith it', said Paul, 'that you are frightened?'

'Frightened of what?' I asked.

'Of the torture of the bithcuitth', said Paul.

Jane smiled. It wasn't easy for her to smile, but she did.

'That's right, love', she said, 'I'm frightened. I'm terrified. I'm scared stiff. I'm really, really frightened.'

TWELVE

Jane went to bed when the children did that night, and fell asleep almost immediately, one arm flung back behind her head and her long hair spread out on the pillow like a pool of water that has caught the sun and winks back gold at the observer.

I went out and across the field through the long grass. The only light on the river was the square of light in the cabin of our boat. I looked back at it and thought about the children, rocked to sleep on the rhythm of the water. I thought about how we had first met, when she had said to me, 'Just because my father's an invalid it doesn't mean I'm looking for a strong and silent Daddy.'

And I had agreed she was doing nothing of the kind. When we crossed roads, though, I noticed, I took her arm, as if she wasn't used to traffic.

I went on up the field and found that there was a road. A small, unmarked lane between two high hedges that wound a course as crazy and dilatory as that of the river. About ten yards down on the other side of the road was a telephone box.

It was the telephone box that reminded me of my father.

Did I say that he had suffered a stroke? Well, he had. I can remember my first sight of him in the hospital – a suddenly cowed old man in the corner of a public ward. Once a charmer, a conjuror, a teller of stories (my mother once said his one aim in life was to upstage his children), he was blasted as a tree is blasted by lightning – one side of him struck away, the other half hanging behind. He looked like some ill-adjusted machine. And all that Spring the good side of him was struggling against the bad side. They took the good side to physiotherapy. They talked to the good side and told it it was feeling better and would soon be walking and talking and standing up to its wicked brother, the bad side, that dribbled stiffly and could not remember the things the good side could remember. The doctors believed, or said they believed, that the good side usually won. That's what they told their patients, anyway. The patients' relatives, too. They didn't tell them about the people they had seen die in that ward or how, sometimes, the bad side won. How, in the end, the bad side always won, for there came a point for all of us when it was no longer possible to be brave and optimistic and good.

I knew, from the moment I spoke to the ward sister, that something was wrong. I had only about sixty pence in change on me. I think I thought I was going to ask one question, how he was, and pass on my love but—

'Mr James,' she said. 'I'm glad you rang. Your mother's here.'

'Yes?' I said.

'Your father's worse,' she said.

'Yes?'

This is, as far as I can recall, exactly what she said.

'In fact he's very much worse, in fact.'

'How much worse?'

'Well,' she said. 'In fact he's dead.'

Looking at it now, on the page, what she said seems cruel, almost comic, but that was not how it seemed at the time. There was something almost touching about her attempts to make his end seem part of some continuum. She prepared her climax like a traditional storyteller. She had an Irish accent, and her inflection   63 seemed to suggest that dying was just one more thing you did, like getting promoted or getting sick and, given time, there was hope of change or recovery from this, the most absolute and final of all human activities.

I can't remember what I said in reply. The money ran out sooner than I expected, perhaps. All I recall is that I stood in the deserted country lane beneath the shadows of the trees, feeling as if gravity had suddenly been suspended. I felt light, very light, as if, had there been a sudden gust of wind, I would have been picked up and blown away, over the fields, back down the sinuous river to the city where my father lay dead.

I know I didn't run back to the boat. I am sure I did not intend to wake anyone up. Their sleep – the sleep of my wife and children – seemed to me so precious that it must not be troubled by such news. I wanted them to be there, on that boat, rocked by the river until it was light again, miraculously, to be greeted by Sam, wildly surprised at its resemblance to the day that had preceded it.

In fact, there was no need to wake Jane. I saw her from about fifty yards. She was standing on the bank, a little way from the boat, gazing out at the fields opposite her. The warmth of the day was still in the air. Her long blonde hair lay down her back. She was naked.

As I watched, she moved forward a little. Although naked she showed no sign of being cold. All her movements had a grace and precision and certainty about them.

I swear that this is what I saw. She knelt at the surface of the river and bowed her head, like some nobleman on the scaffold. For a moment I was reminded of how she looks when she washes her hair over the bath, standing naked, buttocks tilted up, as the nape of the white neck inches forward, and for a moment I was disposed to find this an erotic display. But the steadiness of her actions, the serious tilt of her shoulders and the total emptiness of the scene – dark trees, dark water, dark shape of the boat –

checked any thought of approaching her.

She lowered her hair into the stream and slewed her head this way and that. It wasn't as if she were cleaning herself. She was using her head and her hair like an object. It was as if she were trying to give something back to the river.

When she had finished she stood up and began to squeeze the water out of her hair. She looked now almost fearsomely practical. She could have been a Swedish gym mistress, developing some new sauna technique. After a few minutes she walked back to the boat and clambered up the side. Her nakedness was busy, womanly. She was a model painted by Degas or Renoir – a perfect female form adapted for childbearing, for satisfying others' lusts and, in her time, her own; public and mysterious at the same time. I felt a prickle of desire again. She went in to the cabin and, through the lighted window, I watched her dry herself, towelling her hair vigorously. I could see its gold, worn to near black in the river water, win back its colour in thin streaks of copper, like the beginning of dawn in the sky.

She stood for a moment at the window, looking out at the dark, and I lay where I was in the field, looking back at her image. Then she switched out the lights.

I didn't wake her when I got back to the boat. I didn't tell her about my father until the next morning. And I never told her – never have told her – about how I watched her that night by the river. Like most things never spoken of – this, now, is the first time I have tried to recall it precisely – I sometimes doubt whether I saw it at all.

I left them on the river and went back to London the next morning. The curious thing was that, although I loved my father very much, I did not cry. I didn't cry when I saw him, next morning, stretched out on the hospital bed. I didn't cry at the funeral. Neither did I cry, alone, later, as some people are supposed to do.

I never have cried for my father. And I blame my wife for it. When I try to think of him and her and how I broke the news to her and what she said when she heard, I cannot picture grief. I see her by the Thames, bathing her hair in the stream, naked in an empty field on an English Spring night, while my children slept, yards away.

THIRTEEN

When did I start the story again? Hard to remember. The story is confused now, in my mind, with all the other things that happened. With Jane not eating, for example.

Just as I didn't cry at my father's funeral so she, I am positive about this, refused salmon mayonnaise at the party afterwards. They don't call it a party, do they? They have some tactful word for it – we are too English a family for a wake. My brother and I argued for hours about what wine to choose, much in the way we have always argued about almost every family arrangement. What wine do you choose to demonstrate grief? He was for claret but I finally persuaded him to buy a case of white Rioja.

I have ever since associated white Rioja with death; which hasn't stopped me drinking it.

Jane was standing by the window, next to my mother. The two of them looked, as they usually do, as if they were sharing some sad secret. Perhaps they were both wishing they liked each other better. My brother came up with a plate of salmon, and Jane looked up, abstracted.

'Oh no,' she said. 'No, thank you.'

That was when I realized she had eaten nothing but bread for four days. And she had taken to eating it on her own, while she served the rest of us food. She ate nothing but bread, and not much of that, for two months after my father died.

67

Jane's fast is confused with other things, as well as the story. With the vicar who spoke at my father's funeral, a man who spoke as if he were recommending the deceased for some academic position. With the weather, that changed from the sudden heat we had enjoyed on the river back to the cold easterly winds and showers of harsh rain that we had seen in the weeks before my father died. With the compliments passed on his passing, the shoals of cut flowers under cellophane wrappings and the cards and the notes that accompanied them (many from people I hardly knew), with the fat Polish undertaker, whom my mother praised immoderately for his tact and discretion. So the story itself is confused with the business of eating and of dying.

I couldn't, as it happens, think of an ending for it. It was Jane's comments that had thrown me. I hadn't thought of the story as being anything to do with what she had called 'the nuclear issue' but, once she had suggested it, I could see that it clearly *could be* and, furthermore, could be seen to deal with it in an appallingly crude and explicit fashion. My treatment was in no way mitigated by the fact that I had not realised it *was* about 'the nuclear issue' until Jane pointed it out.

Once I was aware of this fact, the story was impossible to end. The nuclear issue is, like Scheherazade's tales, a story we cannot afford to end. It has to be added to and decorated and refined each time, so that it remains just that – an issue. It spawns fresh characters, new forms of dialogue, sub-plots and false denouéments; because any twist, however tired or absurd, is preferable to the final climax, the one we all wish to avoid.

That didn't stop me telling the story. I told it obsessively in the weeks after my father's death. While Jane shook her head sadly at food, I told the children how the magic pebble was stolen by a group of foreigners from over the border. Of how three brave if elderly white magicians got it back. I went into an enormously long digression on the subject of the black arts, which my eldest son greatly enjoyed. I told them about what happened when a buzzard stole the pebble and flew with it to the far north of the kingdom, where it swallowed the thing, only to be cut open by a simple woodcutter's son called Paul, who carried it back to the capital. I told them—

Well, I told them anything but the real story. I had caught a glimpse of what that would be and of how it ended; and I did not like what I saw.

All through late April and May, while Jane grew steadily thinner and the weather grew steadily worse, I digressed to the children; and visited my opera singer.

I was growing increasingly obsessed with her bottom while she, in her turn, was growing increasingly obsessed with her throat. Once, when we were making love in the *a posteriori* position and I was gazing at her behind, genuinely and sincerely impressed by its pear-shaped regularity, I noticed she was allowing the fingers of one jewelled hand to caress her throat. *My God*, I thought, *do we have anything in common?*

And then, in May, at what should have been the high point of Spring's triumphal entry, we went on a trip, past Tilbury, to the mouth of the Thames. My eldest son was doing a project on the river at his primary school. One group of children had visited the source in the Cotswolds, drawn a picture of Old Father Thames (not, as Jane pointed out, rather remotely, old *Mother* Thames) and traced the river's journey from the sloping hills near Lechlade, down towards Oxford. They had drawn maps and collected pictures of Thames barges and the Royal Swans and the Henley Regatta – in fact, they had images and stories of almost every stretch, apart from the point at which the river died. Nobody at the school seemed very interested in the mouth, the estuary, the end of the river's travels, but I, perhaps because I was born near there, have always loved the landscape east of London, the Marshes, where the convict hulks once lay, the huge upended   *69* oblong of the power station on the Isle of Grain, like some dark pagan temple, and the constantly blurred horizon between land and water that lends a magical touch to the commonest sights, so that container ships seem to be stuck in the middle of fields and the grey, featureless channel to be washing at the feet of distant observers.

There was a brief burst of sunlight as we left, the tightly furled shoots on the late flowering trees in our garden as brilliant as the jewellery my opera singer had clustered round her throat. But by the time we reached the Thames flood barrier rain had come in from the sea, fast moving, mauve squalls of cloud, as if to herald the imminent dissolution of everything out there, joined as it was in one shifting line – land, sea and cloud.

I didn't mind. The Thames estuary was made for grey days.

We took them to the churchyard Dickens described in *Great Expectations* – the pauper graves like white lozenges in the grass. We went on the South side of the river and looked across at Tilbury, where a gigantic Brazilian vessel swung in against the current, to berth at a dock with only a few feet's clearance on either side. And, because the children wanted to see where the river really, *really* ended, we went out to the Isle of Grain and looked out into the dull wastes of the Channel.

'Well,' said Paul, 'where ith it? Where ith the end of the river?'

'There isn't a fence,' I said. 'There isn't an exact place. It's very hard to tell where the river ends and the sea begins.'

I told him about the lightship that is agreed to be the point at which the river ceases but he didn't want to hear about that. He wanted to know the exact point at which the Thames stopped trading. He couldn't believe in a life without precise boundaries. We stood on the wall, down from the power station, looking across at the naked flames of the refinery, the distant northern shore and the thick-waisted ships coming and going in the now steady rain, with the absorbed, private air of visitors to a hospital or a graveyard.

I can't remember when I saw that Jane had gone. One moment she was there, near to me, and the next, when I turned, there was only myself and the three boys and the unfathomable shades of the flat land and the sea. The rain stung my face. I looked over towards the car, parked on a waste lot, off where the road ended. No sign of her. She wasn't along the jetty either, or on the raised promenade behind the wall on which we were standing.

I went back to the car but could not see her anywhere.

The rain was now coming in so fast that the ships out in the Channel had been painted out, and even the menacing lines of the power station behind us had lost their ugly clarity. The rain drove in endlessly, drilling into the children's raw faces, slapping Sam's hair across his forehead, making us gasp with the shock of it, while the land behind us was swamped with grey water, obliterated. It had swallowed Jane like a marsh. She was nowhere to be seen.

'Where'th she gone?' said Paul.

'For a walk,' I said.

The idea seemed ludicrous, but we went back to the car and played out the drama required by my obvious lie. We sat in its steamed-up shell as the rain, prodigal and precise at the same time, repeated its rhythm on the roof, a field of angry clicks, reminding me of when I was a child, when my brother and I had made up one of our eternal quarrels and sat in bed with my father, listening to the rain as he told us stories to quieten us.

'She'll be back in a minute', I said. 'She's just gone to the shops.'

'Tell uth', said Paul, 'the withardth thtory.'

'Yeah', said my eldest son. 'Tell us the wizards one.'

Sam just sat, his eyes wide with wonder, his tiny hands folded over his chest like an alderman at a banquet.

'All right,' I said, 'I'll tell you the story.'

For, suddenly, I had seen how the story ended.

71

FOURTEEN

'Well, the years went by and everyone in the kingdom became very, very good. They were polite to their parents, they never quarrelled and they were kind to those less fortunate than themselves.

Everywhere you went there were white magicians. Everywhere you went people smiled and shared and lived their lives peacefully and well. No one hated his neighbour or wished anyone ill.

I say "no one". There were those, I am afraid, who still felt greedy and spiteful and mean; but they learned to hide their true feelings, and to smile at the people they most hated. They did not dare to act as meanly as they felt, but they waited and watched. Sooner or later, they told themselves, nastiness would become fashionable again.

For this reason the white magician told the king they were not yet ready to pronounce the second charm, the magic word that would unleash the pebble's great power. "We must work", he told him. "We must work and work and work. No one was ever good without trying very hard. And perfect in the search for knowledge? Who knows? That may be a goal we can never reach, for to be both wise and virtuous, cunning and generous, clever and honest, this is the hardest path for anyone to tread."

The person who felt most greedy and spiteful and mean was the white magician's brother. In his heart, although he wore the white magician's robe, now fashionable at court, he was still devoted to the black arts. The moment of human kindness he had felt for his brother had gone; now that his brother was rich and famous and powerful, the black magician hated him more than ever, and thought about nothing apart from how to discover the charm that would give him power over the magic pebble and, hence, over the whole kingdom.

He concealed his true feelings well. He was clever enough to pretend to be ashamed of his evil nature.

"I know", he said to his brother, "that I will never be worthy enough to pronounce the word. I hate myself. All I see when I look in the mirror is how hideous and greedy and selfish I am. I am a truly horrible and disgusting person."

"I know", said his brother, kindly, "I know that."

At this the black magician gave a kind of twitch but quickly recovered and started to whimper to himself as if about the burst into tears.

"I too", went on the white magician, "have awful weaknesses. Why, only the other day I passed a beggar. I didn't give him all my money. I selfishly kept back a couple of pence to buy myself some bread and cheese for my supper. Wasn't that selfish?"

The black magician thought it incredibly stupid. If he saw a beggar he usually aimed a sly kick at him, if he thought no one was watching. And, as for supper, the black magician thought he had a God-given right to smoked salmon every night. Bread and cheese were for other people.'

'He woth greedy', said Paul.

'He was', I said. 'Greedy and selfish and utterly horrible. I hope you never have a brother like that.'

I thought about my own brother. About how different people   *73* said we were. About how once we had fought and now, divided by the conveniences of adult life, we were further apart than anyone I could imagine.

'What did the white magician do next?' asked Tom.

I paused a moment. There had been a time when my white magician was Santa Claus. Once, during the part of the story I told on the boat, he had acquired a Jewish quality. It was all I could do then to stop him shrugging his shoulders and going 'Oy vey!' at every opportunity. Now he was full of the hopeless desire to be good. He reminded me of a Franciscan friar or, in his less convincing moments, the eponymous hero of *Eric, Or Little By Little*. He was small and fine-boned and infinitely sad, like someone who has seen too many terrible things.

'Are you telling uth the thtory?' said Paul.

'Sure', I said. And carried on.

'The black magician did not of course reveal any of his feelings to his brother. Grown-ups become horribly good at lying and not showing their feelings.

"Oh", he said. "You must teach me to be good, dear brother. Please, please, please. . . ."

He became his brother's most promising pupil. And, although they had for many years been far apart they now became inseparable. Night after night he sat up with his brother and talked of their father, long dead, and of their mother, who the black magician referred to as "our dear, dear treasure".

He planned his campaign very carefully. He had deliberately kept up with a few notably odious acquaintances – the Captain of the Guard, for example, who had publicly stated that the white magician should be tortured to give the details of the second charm, in case the pebble should be used by one of the king's enemies while everyone was namby-pambying around trying to be good. The black magician dropped him ostentatiously. He had gone out and caused a few minor disasters or offered to stir up

74

jealousy between two shopkeepers. Now, when people came to him and asked for a little – illegal – black magic, he wept and told them to try and be good. Word soon got around that the black magician was a changed man. But the more he was seen to improve the more he protested his wickedness. He lived all the time in a broom cupboard in his brother's school of white magic, protesting that he was not worthy of anything else. "I am not worthy", he said, "to sleep lying down." He ate nothing but potato peelings and bits of dried custard, left out by the other pupils; and when his brother offered him a pork chop he burst into tears, saying he was not fit for such luxury.

He went to see his widowed mother every month (which, she told a very old friend, was once a month too much). He cleaned her stove for her and bought her new false teeth. He studied white magic very, very hard, and came top in all his lessons, memorizing difficult formulas and devising new and wonderful computations that amazed all who read them.

All the pupils at the school were expected to do white magic homework, but the black magician announced that he would do other people's as well as his own. When the other pupils said they could not possibly let him he became hysterical with grief.

"I am the lowest of the low", he howled. "I am an odious little swine. I am a vile, degraded, horrible little pervert."

"No, you're not", said his fellow pupils, who were beginning to wonder whether he had lost his marbles, "don't be too hard on yourself."

"Am I sanctimonious?" said the black magician. "Am I a goody-goody? Oh no. How disgusting! An odious, hypocritical goody-goody. A whiter than white louse. I have got so long to go before I am halfway decent."

And he fell to weeping so hard that his fellow students had to pat him on the back, and say that, really, he was one of the nicest people they had ever met in their lives.

People, I am sorry to say, were taken in by him. And the most completely deceived was his brother. Like many truly good people, the white magician genuinely believed in his own wickedness. And, when he saw his brother change in front of his eyes, he said to himself, "It has always been easy for me. I have never wanted to be anything but kind and useful. Virtue has been my vice. But my brother is struggling against his own evil nature. Perhaps he is the one who should rule over the pebble."

The fact that a little bit of him did not like this idea only made him the more determined to pursue it. He put his doubts down to jealousy of his brother's new-found skills in the arts of white magic, and the more real pain he felt at the prospect of telling his brother the second charm the more it seemed to him that that was precisely what he should do.

"True goodness", he told himself, "is *hard*."

The black magician had now taken to living in a public lavatory near to the school and refusing all food apart from the most unpleasant-looking potato peelings that could be found. He scarcely slept at all, and was growing thinner and thinner. He spent long hours talking to the white magician about their early lives.

"I can never forgive myself", he said, "for calling our dead dear father 'Old Bignose'. How I miss him now he is gone! How I cry for him night after night!"

As the weeks and the months passed, the thought grew in the white magician's mind that, at long last, he might be looking at someone who was perfect in the search for knowledge, a man fit to pronounce the second charm that would unleash all the power of the magic pebble. For, he told himself, he is struggling to learn goodness as well as the white crafts of which I am so proud. And is not the struggle for knowledge knowledge itself?

He and everyone else could not see that they were about to

place the pebble into the hands of one who was unworthy and, if they were not careful, the kingdom, the lands around it, everything they had ever known would be most horribly destroyed.

Virtue can be quite as dangerous as evil, and disasters are often the result of good intentions.

The white magician announced that his brother was to be given the pebble, and that he himself would teach him the magic word that would give them all good fortune, health, happiness and the secure provision of all their needs.

When I have the pebble, thought the black magician, *then you will all obey me. And it won't be me who's sleeping in broom cupboards and lavatories.'*

FIFTEEN

'I expect', I said to the children, 'that you want to know what the second magic spell was.'

'Yeth,' said Paul. 'We do. And we want to know the firtht one an' all.'

'Of course,' I said, 'I can't tell you.'

'Why not?'

Paul has all the compact charm of a small gorilla. His blonde hair just above his eyes, he met my gaze in the driving mirror and would not let it go.

'Well,' I said, 'some magic charms are so powerful they are dangerous. People should not be told about them.'

'Like what?' said Paul.

'Like E=mc squared,' I said.

This, for some reason, made them laugh hysterically.

'My God,' said my eldest son, 'E=mc squared. Really weird, man.'

'What I mean is,' I went on, 'we might be better off not knowing some things. Sometimes scientific knowledge can be dangerous.'

'Right,' said my eldest son glumly. 'Like nuclear weapons, for a start.'

78

Before I had a chance to answer this, Paul said, 'It'th alwayth good to know thingth.'

'Yes,' I said.

Sam leaned forward in his seat, his tiny hands gripping my back.

'What did the wizard do?' he said.

'I'll tell you,' I said.

And so I continued, as the rain beat its ceaseless argument on the roof and the light bled away from the flat landscape.

'It was agreed that the white magician would tell the black magician the magic word of power that would enable the magic pebble to go to work and solve all the problems of the world.'

'Or to blow to bits,' said my eldest son. 'If the black magician was not perfect in the search for knowledge.'

'Which he motht thertainly wath not,' said Paul. 'In fact he wath exthtremely *evil*.'

I felt that the story was no longer under my control. I look at the rain lashing the windows of the car and held up my hand for silence.

'Can I continue, please?'

A silence. At last, I continued.

'Of course,' I said, 'I can't tell you what the words were. But as you can imagine they were extremely secret and complicated and it took the black magician three weeks to learn the second word of power. Even then, as it was an extremely long word, longer even than antidisestablishmentarianism, he sometimes got it wrong.

The white magician wasn't worried about that side of things. What worried him was that he did not quite know what the magic pebble would *do*, when the second charm was pronounced. Would it need a lot of space? Would it, perhaps, rise up in the air? Or bore a hole in the ground?

Once his brother was word-perfect in the spell the white magician persuaded the king to build a wooden platform on a level plain, some miles to the west of the capital. The pebble was placed on a mauve cushion in the middle of the platform, guarded by the crack troops of the king's own regiment.

The day on which the word was to be pronounced was declared a public holiday. Tickets to watch the white magician's brother perform were sold at an enormous price. Families began to gather, at first light, to watch the spectacle, although very few of them had much idea of what precisely it was that they were about to see. Some said they were about to witness a hanging. Others were convinced that someone important was about to get married, although none of them could agree as to who the happy couple were.

By ten in the morning of that fine, clear Summer's day there were thousands and thousands of people littering the surface of the plain. Children played ball games, mothers fed babies, stalls selling drinks and refreshments crowded around the magnificent platform. Then, on the far horizon, people saw a cloud of dust. The king and his two most trusted magicians were approaching.

The white magician and his brother were both dressed from head to foot in white linen.

It has to be said that the black magician's squinting eyes, misshapen nose, enormous red ears and rubbery lips made him look a little like a gremlin or deformed monkey wrapped in swaddling clothes. As he cringed his way up the platform people close enough to make out his features were amazed that anyone so well-known for being good should look so repulsive.

"True goodness," mothers told their children, "comes from inside. Appearances are not important." Although this did not stop those same mothers from telling these same children not to chew their coat cuffs and for heaven's sake stop spilling food down their fronts.

The black magician stepped up to the cushion and the king held up his hand for silence.

"Today," he said, "is a great day for all of us."

The black magician's beady little eyes were fixed on the pebble. People some distance away from the platform began to ask what had happened to the gallows, while others, even further away, waved handkerchiefs at the distant figures, asking each other earnestly which was the bride and which the groom.

"Magic", said the king, "is an unstoppable force."

But I will not bore you with the king's speech. It was, even by the average standards of royal eloquence, a disappointing affair. He went on for hours about how much better things had been since he became king and how much incredibly better they were going to be Now We Had the Pebble.

And, all the time, the black magician eyed it, as it lay, indifferent, on the cushion.

Any minute now, he thought, *and it is mine.*

When the King had finished, the Grand Vizier spoke, and when he had finished the white magician spoke, and when he had finished—'

'*What happened,*' said Paul, '*when he thaid the thpell?*'

My heart wasn't in this story: they could tell. I swivelled round in the seat and turned to look at my three sons. The rain drummed on the roof and I thought again *where's she gone?*

'When he said the spell—'

'Which you can't tell us,' said my eldest.

'Becauth,' said Paul, 'if there wath a pebble in the car it would exthplode.'

'When he said the spell—'

I was almost shouting.

'*When he said the spell the pebble started to hum. And to spin. And to glow. And it didn't stop. And as it spun a hard white light gathered round it, like the halo of a saint you might see in the stained-glass window of some church. And that light, very slowly, started to grow. It swelled outwards, inch by inch, like a sponge in water; but, unlike a* 81 *sponge, it kept going. It grew and grew until for miles around it could be seen – a huge ball of light, shining as strongly and fiercely as the sun, so that the king, his courtiers and the two magicians looked like figures walking through fire.'*

SIXTEEN

'When it had swollen to the size of a small cathedral—', I continued.

'How big's that?' said Tom, in his best earnest elder-brother manner.

'When it was seven hundred yards wide and eight hundred yards long,' I said, 'it exploded. Not like a bomb going up but like a huge wet soap bubble you've made in the bath. It made a noise like a gigantic fart. And all over the plain, and over most of the people there (apart, as it happened, from the two magicians) fell tiny scraps of what looked like white powder. People brushed it off their hair and shoulders, and found that it smelled sweet, rather like lemon mixed with sugar. They licked it off their finger then and found that it didn't taste as sweet as it smelled. It tasted sour and musty. In fact it was a bit like eating old football boots. They were chewy, too, like toffee, and the bits stuck to your teeth.

None of the officials on the platform knew what to make of this. They had been told that whatever happened was going to do the kingdom (by which they meant *themselves*) a great deal of good. And so they puffed out their chests and waved their arms and made speeches about how brilliant and fantastic everything was going to be from now on. They confided in each other too, while the speeches were going on, in the way very important people do.

"Of course I said to the Assistant Chief Gardener last *March* . . ." you could hear them mutter, or "I said to the king's speech-writer *and he agreed with me* that the pebble . . ." *Et cetera et cetera.* For all the world they looked like a crowd of turkeys, fluffing out their feathers, for no reason at all except that it made them feel good.

As for the pebble, no one could find it anywhere. The only sign that it had ever existed were these white fragments, falling like snow on a winter's morning.

After there had been hours of speeches and applause everybody packed up and went home. Many people were still unsure about what the whole ceremony had been about, but there was general agreement that the bride had looked lovely and that the beasts who had been executed got no less than they deserved. As for the white flakes – after a few days they turned bright mauve and started to froth quietly to themselves. But as by this time the only people anywhere near the plain or the deserted platform were the cleaners it was not considered important.

Now the king's eldest daughter was called Thomasina—'

'Like me,' said Tom.

'No, no, no,' I said, 'nothing like you. Her name wasn't Thomasina actually. It was Lynda. Lynda with a Y, which I am sure you will agree is a very stupid way of spelling Linda. Anyway, the king's eldest daughter ate an exceptionally large amount of the white stuff that floated down from the sky after the pebble exploded. In fact she had collected the flakes in a handkerchief, and had not allowed anyone else to get near her supply, so that, when she gobbled up her harvest, she didn't just lick the odd flake off her fingers but poured the stuff on to a plate and made a proper meal of it, adding a little sugar for luck. She told her family it tasted like cinnamon and raspberry jam, and the king, who like everyone else was still waiting for good things to come from the pebble, thought that at any moment there would be another shower of flakes, after which nobody would have to grow corn or raise chickens or any of the other boring things of which he was supposed to be in charge. *Perhaps*, thought the king, *those flakes will make my daughter beautiful or charming or musical or clever or thin* (she was exceptionally fat) *or good at languages or generous or fun to be with*. Any one of these qualities would have done something to make the king's daughter a more bearable child.

For a few days, however, the girl showed no sign of change whatsoever. She continued to loaf about the palace, eating crisps and playing with her brother's computer. But, on the third day, when she was getting ready for school, she noticed that she would not fit into her school clothes. When the court tailor measured her he found that the king's eldest daughter had put on half an inch. But not half an inch round the waist or neck or thighs – half an inch *all over*. She had grown the way a bubble grows, as if something were trying to force its way out.

Nobody took any notice. The black magician was busy holding huge parties and telling all the right people exactly how and why and where all the troubles of the kingdom would end, while his brother, who was beginning to have doubts about whether the black magician had been entirely honest with him, stood at the edge of these occasions, waiting and watching and worrying.

Meanwhile, upstairs, in her suite of rooms, Lynda with a Y grew and grew and grew. The first week she put on half an inch all over. The second week two inches all over. And on the third four inches. In the fourth week she was too fat to get out of her room to see the court physician. And by the fifth week she had put on sixteen inches all over.

After that she started swell uncontrollably. Like dough rising or a balloon filling with gas, she got fatter and fatter until her features – never very clear at the best of times – entirely disappeared and her fingers, her nose, her ears, toes and elbows and knees were mere plump points in a sea of skin.

On the fortieth day of her illness, when she was thirty-eight feet across and twenty-nine feet high, the court physician said she had something called Circular Disease. Do you know what circular disease is?'

'No', said Paul.

'Circular Disease is an illness in which the patient aspires to the condition of a circle. And the court physician explained to the royal family that, when the crown princess was forty feet from end to end at every point, she could be said only to have a diameter and a surface and to have reached the *critical point* of circular disease after which there was no time to be lost in getting her into some other shape.'

'Like a thquare,' said Paul.

'Right,' I said. 'That is how you cure circular disease. You turn the person into a square, then into a rectangle, then into a triangle and then into a straight line, and then you pull out the straight line in various directions until the person looks like a person again. This is what they proposed to do with the king's daughter. They knocked down the walls of her room and carried her up to the roof of the castle. On the forty-third day of her illness she was forty feet in diameter.

"Now," said the court physician, "we begin the treatment."

But the king's eldest daughter was swelling up faster and faster, and it was too late for the protractors, set-squares, rulers, compasses and dividers that were all waiting in a sterile bath for the treatment of circular disease. Her clothes had long since been torn off by her expanding flesh, and, as the court physician approached her with a pair of dividers, she reached a diameter of fifty-two feet and a total surface area of pi-r squared × 2 (or something like that), which was the point at which she exploded.

Fragments of what looked like white crystals showered down on those waiting round the crown princess's bedside, but this time they were not snowflakes, they were alive. They were a crowd of small, angry white ants. They buzzed and hummed and seemed to glow as they spun tiny angry circles in the air. And the first person they bit was the court physician.'

'Then *he* thwelled up,' said Paul.

'No,' I said. 'He did no such thing. In fact he was perfectly all right. Apart from the deep sense of remorse he felt at the cack-handed way he had tackled his first-ever case of Circular Disease he was fine. And then, a few days later, he felt a little dizzy. That night, he told his wife, his eyes hurt him and he felt weightless. Three days later he was dead. On the last day before he died he was delirious and screamed and screamed and screamed. Although he could not speak, those around him said that it was as if he could see some hideous thing there on the bed beside him, some shape as dark and fearful as fear itself. He screamed right up until the end, and when he died his face was blasted with fear, blasted as a tree when struck by lightning.

That was when the plague started. Carried by the vicious white ants that had sprung out of the remnants of the king's hideous daughter, they buzzed and bit and spun circles and hummed like a huge top as they swarmed from the end of the kingdom to the other. And they carried plague wherever they went.

It was the worst plague anyone had ever known. It killed the rich and the poor, the meek and the proud, the good and the bad. It killed at court, in the street, in the huts of peasants, on the roads and the great rivers, on ships at sea. In two weeks the sickness had spread to neighbouring kingdoms. Every day, all day, in private and in public, people died. Bodies lay on street corners like sacks of wheat waiting to be loaded. Death was only of incidental importance. Those who survived made hard, clever jokes. No one mourned their loved ones. There were no loved ones. You simply could not afford to love. People died, whether you loved them or not.

87

"Listen", said the king to the white magician, just as his second daughter had come down with the plague, "I thought you said our troubles were all going to *end* when this pebble got to work."

"End or begin", said the white magician, "according to whether the person saying the magic word was perfect in the search for knowledge or was a horrible deceitful little person only out for his own good."

"Yes", said the king, "I see . . .' and he looked meaningfully at the black magician who was shifting nervously from foot to foot in the corner of the room. Indeed, since the beginning of the plague the black magician had not spoken much about the pebble – or if he had mentioned it he had usually referred to it as "something my brother was rather keen on . . ." or "a project we got involved with some years ago . . .".

"Why's everyone looking at me?" said the black magician. "*He* found the thing in the first place."

And so it was that both brothers were thrown into the deepest, darkest dungeon in the kingdom which, it turned out, was the

safest place to be, because there were no white ants there. Here
they argued about whose fault it was. When they were bored
with that they argued about all the other things they usually
argued about, such as their father's funeral (at which the black
magician had insisted on serving lemon tea, for some reason
known only to himself), about their respective careers, about

sport, science, literature – everything in fact you could imagine. When they had finished arguing they fought, as they had fought when children, kicking and punching and screaming and howling. And when they had finished with fighting they fell asleep.

While they were asleep a beautiful woman with long blonde hair appeared in their cell. Although her hair was dripping wet, as if she had been bathing it in some unpolluted river, the rest of her was bone-dry. She passed one hand over the black magician and he slept more soundly; then she passed a hand over the white magician, and he awoke and stared her in the face, and knew at once that he was not dreaming, that this was no less than the woman who had given him the pebble.

She bent down very close to him, and she smelt very sweet. To his surprise her hair was no longer wet. It was dry and soft, like sweet grass in a meadow by a river. He put up his hand to touch it. She took his palm between her two hands and said, in a gentle voice, "I will tell you who I am and how it is I came by the pebble and how it is this terrible curse may yet be lifted. You will have to be very, very brave but you may yet rescue your people from this terrible affliction."

"Tell me," said the white magician, "tell me how the prophecy may be undone. Tell me where this magic is from and how we may run it backwards – if any can turn back time or wipe out wickedness, once committed."

So she sat there on the filthy floor of his cell and she told him her story.'

SEVENTEEN

'She wath a witch,' said Paul.

'How did you know?' I said.

'She woth obviouthly a witch,' he said. 'Thinth she arrived magically.'

I stopped and looked back out into the flat Thames landscape for any sign of my wife. There was none. *My God*, I thought, *she's right. What am I teaching them? To hate and fear women? And is there any other way for a man to tell a story?*

'She *was* a witch,' I said, 'but not a serious witch. A witch by upbringing.'

'How do you mean?' said my eldest.

'She was brought up by a wizard. I mean, she was actually a wizard's daughter. And it was the wizard who gave her the pebble. He was incredibly evil.'

This wasn't much better though, was it? My story now presented women as the pretty but evil accomplices of men. This was actually worse. If I was going to give this story a feminist, nuclear twist, I would have to invent a huge earth-mother goddess, who came to the rescue. Maybe a creature with five breasts could lumber up out of the tundra and squirt milk into the white ants and destroy them. Or maybe a young female student of white magic could arrive on the scene and talk some sense into the king. Or—

I looked back into their faces, as hungry for knowledge as the magician in my story, and said, 'The wizard's name was Schlock. He lived in the far north of the country near where the black and white magician were born. He was extremely evil. He hated all human beings, but especially girls and women. You see, he had six daughters and he had always wanted a son. And he hated his daughters worst of all.'

'Blimey,' said my eldest son.

Paul did not, as he sometimes would, side with Schlock. He had too much sense to side with a bad wizard, especially one who lived in the far north, even if Schlock, very sensibly, hated girls. Maybe, I could see his small, serious face thinking, the girls Schlock hated were okay.

'That's why', I said, 'the King's eldest daughter was the first to die in the plague.'

'Right,' said my eldest son, with what sounded like relief at such congruity. I was somewhat relieved by it myself.

'There were six of these pebbles,' I went on, 'and they were all hidden in various places in the kingdom. Some in the mountains, one in the king's palace, and one in the river, which was the one the white magician had found—'

'One in a lavatory,' said Paul.

'Yes,' I said, 'one in a lavatory.'

'I know,' said my eldest, 'the white magician had to find the other five pebbles and then the charm would be broken and the plague would stop.'

'You think?' I said.

I didn't like to admit that this was an option I had considered. *Even if we no longer share a God*, I thought, *we share these stories, don't we? These fragments of old tales and myths, propped up against our ruin, all we have to ward off a future that is less like a ball of light, more a gradual creeping darkness, coming in over the fields, clogging our powers of speech and thought. There are no longer any stories for children, since the horrors we share are so simple.*

'Yes,' went on my eldest, 'and the white magician had to sort of undergo *tests* to find the pebbles and the woman with the long hair was a sort of *good* witch and they sort of *teamed up* to find them, sort of thing.'

This was beginning to sound like some piece of social realist agitprop. I didn't think the woman with the long hair, assuming she was just a woman and not a disguise assumed by some dreadful creature, was the sort to team up with anyone.

'No,' I said, 'the other five pebbles were never found. They never have been found. The woman with the long hair had no idea of where they were. She only knew about her pebble which had been given to her by her father—'

'Schlock,' interposed Paul.

'Maybe not', I said. 'Maybe his name wasn't Schlock. Maybe no one will ever know his name. But he had given her the pebble years ago when she was playing by the river. Not a river like it is here, wide and strong, but a clear stream high up, near the beginnings of a mountain. . . .'

I looked out at the rain-sodden landscape once again.

'How did he give her the pebble?' asked my eldest.

Sam was lost. He too stared out at the rain. He did not blink. His expression was one of total, objective, one might almost have said *scientific* absorption. The plague and the deaths had lost him – as it was, perhaps, better that they should; for dying is so little like magic, the very young cannot understand it at all.

'If you'll let me tell the story,' I said, 'I'll tell you. This woman was the sixth daughter of an evil wizard.'

'What was she called?' said Sam, suddenly.

'Jane,' I said.

This gave them pause for thought.

'Like Mum,' said Paul, brightly.

'Yes,' I said, 'but let me tell her story the way she told it, this woman with the long hair, miles underground, with the ugly misshapen black magician asleep on the floor and no noise to be heard but the rustle of the rats in the next door cell, and her clear, low voice, running on like the river near which she was born.'

They were quite silent. I went on.

'"My father," the woman told the white magician, "was an evil magician and greatly feared by all those around. I and my five sisters hated and feared him, for at his pleasure he could make us assume any shape he wanted and suffer all the torments he was pleased to bestow upon us.

"He was evil, but very, very cunning, and he wanted to know all the secrets of the Universe. He wanted to know, above all, how things worked. What it was that made trees flower or shed their leaves. What thing it was that *worked* – people, plants, streams. He thought, you see, there was some trick, or secret, like a pulley or a coil, some machine, at the heart of each thing in the world, and if he could only get at the machine and pull it to bits and understand it then he would have power over the object he had studied.

"The wish to know was not a simple wish, you understand. Once he knew how something worked – whether it was a flower or a waterfall or a human being – he would not let it be. He would crouch by the waterfall or flower and try to stop it and start it at his pleasure, as if it were some engine he had devised. If it was a stream he would cause it to flow or cease at his command. If it was a tree, to bud or droop, like a dog is taught to beg for food. If it was a human being he would start it and stop it thinking or talking or breathing or walking or crying. Human beings were most fun because there was no end to the things they could be made to do.

"But it was dead things that fascinated him most of all. It was easy to cut open a human or tear a flower to pieces. But a pebble!

A piece of rock! A diamond or a vein of gold! Those hard, immovable things, older than any animal, who have brothers and sisters on the moon and the more distant planets.

"And they too, you must believe me, have souls and guardians. Stones cry out sometimes, when people tear at their secrets and seek to find out the things that bind them or force them apart.

"It is a strange thing to say, but my father tortured stones. He assaulted the rocks of the earth, like some inquisitor in search of

information, of what and if and how and when. But the poor dumb pebbles, like creatures with only simple faith, would not give in to him.

"For we lived by a river, and it was the pebbles in the stream he heated and cooked, cracked and tore, shredded and powdered, thought about ceaselessly. And perhaps it was his thoughts that were the worst, for what he wanted was not merely to know but to make those same stones obey him the way the trees and the flowers and the streams and we, his unhappy daughters, obeyed him.

"There must, he was convinced, be some soft and yielding thing about these pebbles. And so he conjured over them, ceaselessly, in search of what he always called *the heart of the thing*, waiting for the moment when he might have mastery over the dead things of the earth, as well as the living.

"One night three men came to him. They had no eyes and their skin was as white as mushroom caps. They were wearing clothes the colour of clay, and their hands were chapped and raw, as if they had been mining precious metal, deep in the earth. When they spoke their voices rang like the side of a spade striking a stone. They cursed my father. They cursed his magic and his cruelty. And they gave him six pebbles. Six perfect pebbles.

" 'This', they said, 'is how you and all human kind are cursed. And most especially cursed are the ones you call wise, the magicians and the ones who seek after knowledge, which to us is no knowledge, rather a painful infliction we must bear. And as you seek power over the earth so shall the earth seek power over you. If any mortal man, however powerful, finds one of these pebbles, then to this man and not to you shall the pebble give up its secret. And, if this man be not perfect in the search for knowledge, then the very stones will rise up and destroy the earth that you have so plundered and tormented.'

"So my father hid the six pebbles. Not, you understand,

96

because he feared for the earth, but because he feared a man *perfect in the search for knowledge.* And wished that no one should have the power if he did not possess it. And he set his six daughters each to guard a pebble, and commanded them, each with a riddle of her own, to warn any that sought for her pebble to understand to what great harm it might lead. Which was why I told to you the rhyme –

At the first word the pebble will hum and spin.

At the second our troubles will end or begin.

"For only when we have mastery over all things *and also know how to rule them wisely* then will all our troubles end."

"But we aren't perfect are we?" said the white magician, "in the search for knowledge or anything else for that matter? Is this how it all ends? When we try to find out something or *do* something, why does it always end like this? Are we supposed to leave the world alone – just wander around, chewing the grass like goats? Is everything we try to make doomed to end like this?"'

EIGHTEEN

It was then that I saw Jane.

She was standing in the rain, a few yards away from the passenger window-seat. She made no effort to approach the car. She wasn't looking in my direction, but out towards the river and the sea. All I could see was her long hair, soaked with the rain. I leaned over, wound down the window and called to her.

At first she didn't answer. Then she turned, very slowly, and, when I saw her face, marked by rain as if by tears, I thought for a moment I had dreamed her appearance. For she looked to me then the way she had looked when I had first met her, like a Burne-Jones Ophelia. I found myself thinking – *it's not exactly that I don't love her. It's that I've wasted the love there was between us. If you don't take care of love it goes.*

'Are you having fun out there?'

She walked towards the car, climbed in and slammed the door after her.

'Are you okay?' I said.

'Fine,' she said. 'Fine.'

There was silence. In the back seat the children began to play a quiet, complicated game. They knew that some adult history was being related. Nothing to do with them.

'You're not eating,' I said.

'No,' she said.

Another silence. Then she said –

'Ano-re-xia. . . .'

She said this in a deep humorous voice.

'I'm not eating,' she said, 'when I'm with you.'

'Oh,' I said.

'I eat okay,' said Jane, 'but not with you.'

'Ah.'

Another silence.

'I don't love you,' she said. 'I've stopped loving you.'

I didn't know what to say, so I said nothing.

'I don't want to share food with you, you see. I don't want to share stories with you. I don't want to share my life with you. I don't want you any more.'

I cleared my throat. When I did speak, I thought I sounded like a rather bad lawyer I had hired to conduct my defence, inadequately briefed, incredibly tactless, nervous of the judge, unaware of the finer points at issue. And then I thought, *Defence? What am I defending? Is it that I still love her?*

'Why's that?' I said.

'It's not your affairs,' she said. 'I've stopped bothering about those. And about your attempts to conceal them. It's you. You've become hard. And you're cautious and complacent now, which you weren't when I married you. You're just another stupid little Englishman with his usual bloody cold.'

'Sorry?'

'You know. *L'Anglais avec son sang-froid habituel.* The Englishman with his usual bloody cold. The world seems to hurt you so much you arm yourself against it. And so you stop feeling. And so . . .'

I coughed elaborately.

'Where did you go,' I said, 'that day at Greenwich?'

'Where do you think I went?'

'I don't know,' I said.

She looked at me sideways. *I don't know her*, I thought. *I don't know who she is or what she feels.*

'I've got someone else,' she said.

'Oh.'

Curiously enough, I didn't find this in any way surprising. *Of course*, I thought. It was something I had always known, it occurred to me, but had never bothered to think about.

'Do you want to know about him?'

'Not really,' I said. 'Is he called Kevin?'

'No,' she said.

'I thought he might be,' I said. 'Or if not Kevin something like Kevin. I thought he might be non-sexist and non-racist and care about the world and nuclear weapons and all of that.'

She didn't answer this.

'I'd had a shower,' she said. 'That's why my hair was wet.'

'Yes,' I said. 'I suppose you'd been fucking him.'

She shrugged. I went on. I didn't like the sound of my voice, but I went on.

'You'd had a fuck and a shower and although your hair was wet you couldn't be bothered to make up a story, you probably thought *"he'll* make up the story. He seems to be making up stories at the moment—". Although, come to think of it, I've always made up stories, haven't I? About where I'd been or who I'd been with. Only difference about these stories was – they were for . . .'

Who were they for? I didn't know. Children or adults? Or were they for a dead man? A seventy-one-year-old journalist, whose body was burned to ashes in a crematorium in West London, and scattered over the polite green lawns that surrounded it. Were they for someone who would never hear them, who wouldn't even begin to understand them if he did? What was the point in *101* the stories anyway? What was the use of them?

There was another long silence. I noticed that the children, too, were silent. They must have been listening to what we were saying. *Well, let them*, I thought. *Let them find out what the world is like. They'll find out soon enough. Why not now?*

I don't think Jane was aware of the children at all. She sat, straight-faced, next to me, looking like someone reading from a prepared text.

'I want a divorce,' she said.

'Sure,' I said.

It's important not to let them see they're hurting you. Don't let them see how vulnerable you are. Come on hard. Rock hard. Right?

'I suppose', I said, 'you'll want the children.'

I thought I said this pretty well. *You'll want the children. And the house. Fine. Anything else? Perhaps I could have that small green tin in the bathroom cupboard? You gave it to me in Jugoslavia. Remember? Sentimental value. No? Fine.*

I'll say this for women – they're not sentimental about objects, about things. They know that they have their value, like everything else.

She turned to me. 'Do you want them?'

I realized she was talking about our children. I looked up at the driving mirror. They were arranged in a neat row, listening to our conversation, in the attitudes they might have taken up if listening to a story. Oh, and what a story, eh? Our lives are a moral obscenity to our children, since they so flagrantly contradict what we teach them. We eat flesh and tell them to love animals. We tell them to practise peace and all our lives offer them war as an example. How can they be expected to make sense of us, and so of themselves?

Sometimes I think it is only through stories we can reach them. I had a vision of myself and my three sons living somewhere, like children. *We'll leave the sauce bottle on the table*, I thought, *and I'll tell them stories.*

At the same time I saw how utterly apart from them I had grown. I was merely an entertaining stranger.

'You see, you're quite charming,' she said. 'But do you think you could do what I do? Clean them and nag them and feed them and make yourself disliked by them for their sake?'

There was silence. I lowered my head.

'I could try.'

Another silence.

'You've always been a child-father, haven't you? You haven't taken the strain, have you? You pick them up and put them down at your leisure. And when it suits you you tell them stories, to amuse yourself as much as them.'

'You're right, of course,' I said.

I was now feeling less like a defence lawyer than a condemned man. *They can't do this to me. Oh yes they can, chum.*

'I quite liked your story, actually,' she said.

'Yes?'

'Yes. It was like you. It was picked up from here and there, but held together by charm and a sort of directness. It was engaging. Like you.'

She turned towards me.

'But you don't make any kind of sense any more.'

I coughed again. 'What kind of sense?'

'I don't know. Moral sense.'

'You sound like my father.'

She looked at her hands. She was twisting them this way and that. Outside, the rain kept coming.

'What are we doing?' said my eldest son.

'We're going home,' I said.

I started the engine and turned the car away from the sea.

'Go on with the withardth thtory', said Paul.

'Mum doesn't like it,' I said.

'It's good, actually,' said my eldest son.

'I don't mind it,' said Jane.

We bumped back on to the road and drove back towards the power station.

'It's near the end anyway', I said.

'Finish it off then,' said Jane. 'For Christ's sake, finish it off.'

'All right,' I said.

As she sat beside me, silent, looking out first at the marshes, and later at the grey south eastern fringes of the capital where I was born, I finished my story.

NINETEEN

"'Look at your brother," said the woman with the long hair. "Asleep on the floor."

The white magician looked at his brother.

"Is he a good person?" she went on.

"No", said the white magician. "He's completely and utterly disgusting. He's rude and greedy and selfish and conceited. And he never lets me sit next to the window on a long train journey. He's vile. I thought he'd made up his mind to be perfect but it turns out he planned on staying horrible all the time."

Imprisonment had sharpened the white magician's tongue.'

Now, I thought, my magician was about six or seven. He wasn't like any of my children. He was like me when I was small. Outwardly I think I was a very grave, composed child, but inside I was humming as viciously as the ants in my story. I was jealous of my older brother. I think that was it. I looked sideways at Jane. Her big, slumbrous features were turned away from me, away from all of us, out at the interminable rain.

I've never really known her, I thought, *I've never really engaged with her.*

"'It's all black and white to you, isn't it?" said the woman with the long hair.

"What do you expect?" said the white magician. "I'm a *white magician*, in case you hadn't noticed. So, as my brother is a *black* magician, the world looks pretty *black and white* as far as I'm concerned. Okay?"

"There is only one way to cure the plague", said the woman. "Do you know what it is?"

"Should I offer myself as a sacrifice and commit suicide?" said the white magician.

The woman looked at him sideways. "What a completely ridiculous idea," she said. Then she sat on the stone flags of the cell. Her long blonde hair fell in the dirt on the floor. She tugged hard at her fringe and the whole of the front of her scalp came away. Underneath the long blonde hair she was as bald as an egg.

She didn't stop there. She tugged at her nose too, and that came away in her hand, to reveal a small, rather red nose stuck with black hairs. Then she pulled at her cheeks. First one, then the other, and underneath her beautiful white skin she had a bristly black beard and a mouth full of badly fitting false teeth. Her voice was changing too. Instead of a ghostly, magical poetic sort of voice she now sounded like a grocer with a head cold.

"What good would that do?" she, or rather *it*, said.

"Don't take anything else off," said the magician. "I don't think I could stand it. I don't think I know what's what any more."

"You certainly don't," said the bearded creature. "If you think committing suicide is going to stop a plague you must be bonkers."

"I don't know," said the white magician, peeved by her attitude. "Stranger things have happened. All this happened because of a magic *pebble*, for God's sake."

"Pebble?" said the little bearded man. "What pebble?"

"What do you mean, what pebble?" said the magician. "The pebble all this is about. In case you hadn't noticed."

"I hadn't," said the bearded man, tugging at his ears. "I came in late to this story. All I know is, there's a plague and people are dying and you and your brother here are two rather intelligent people doing nothing about it but arguing about the stupidest things. That is, when you're not blathering about pebbles."

"Listen," said the white magician, "I am a magician and—"

"I don't care", interrupted the man, "if you're the Akond of Swat. I don't care if you're Shakin' Stevens or one of the Beastie Boys, frankly. All I know is, there's a plague and you're supposed to be an intelligent person and you're not doing anything about it. It's your duty to do something about it."

"How?" said the white magician.

"Use your loaf," said the little man. "And your mince pies. And wake up your brother and talk to him about it. He may be a loathsome little creep but he's your brother and he's rather clever. The only way you'll get anywhere in this world is by working with intelligent people. And spending time with your family."

The white magician sniffed. He was about to start a speech about knowledge and science and sacrifice and pebbles, but it all seemed unimportant now. The one thing he did know was that he didn't want to spend time with his brother.

"You see," said the little man, who had now taken off both ears and was starting on his beard, "your brother may not be all that bad. After all, what made him a black magician in the first place? You let it happen, didn't you? My God, it's probably your fault he's so evil and twisted. You get all the kind words and everyone likes you and says you're a terribly nice person, while he gets all the abuse and rubbish. Maybe you were too much of a goody-goody when you were kids. I bet you sucked up to your Mum and Dad something rotten from the look of you. Do you ever talk about these things with a qualified person? In my view you need psychiatric help."

"Listen," said the white magician, "I don't like all this—"   *107*

"You," said the bearded man, "are someone who doesn't like facing up to things. That is obvious. And what you had better face up to now is what is in front of you. And what's in front of you, my lad, is a particularly nasty species of ant."

So saying, he began to peel off the last of his beard. It wasn't just his beard that came away. It was the skin and the hair on his head too. He unwound himself like an apple being peeled, and as beard and hair gave way to skin and skin unfolded, from head to shoulders to chest to legs, the white magician found he was looking at a large white oval creature, with eight legs and two long, waving probosci. He was indeed looking, and indeed talking to and at, a particularly nasty species of ant.

"Go on," said the ant. "Think how you could put a stop to me." And it laughed – a nasty, conceited cackling sort of laugh.

At this point, the black magician woke up. "Ugh," he said to his brother. "An ant."

"Not just any ant," said the Ant, "but the Head Ant."

"Go away," said the black magician.

"Shan't," said the ant.

The black magician threw his shoes at it, spat at it, threw bits of the cell at it, did any number of ghastly things but the ant was not affected in any way. It lay on the floor of the cell, waving its feelers and smirking. Eventually the black magician sidled up to it, and, holding his magician's cap in one hand, said in his soapiest, most ingratiating voice, "Can't we be friends?"

"You don't fool me," said the ant.

"Please?" said the magician.

By way of answer the ant lifted up its left front leg and, from something that looked rather like a fleshy tap, just underneath where its scales began, squirted a stream of brown juice at the black magician. His aim was good, but missed. For, as well as being repulsive, the black magician was extremely agile.

The brown juice splashed into the wall of the cell and dripped and showered off it to form a large steaming puddle, which smelled of old socks and school lavatories. The white magician was about to try to sweep it away but his brother warned him not to go anywhere near it.

"It's bound to be poisonous", he said. Being a black magician, you see, he knew exactly how unpleasant creatures like the ant operated.

"Too right it's poisonous," said the ant proudly. "It's plague juice." And he cackled unpleasantly.

"Kill anyone, that would," he went on. "Young and old, rich and poor, famous and obscure no problem. You name it, it kills it."

"Anything except ants, I suppose," said the black magician.

"Oh no," said the ant in a self-satisfied voice. "This is the real stuff, this is. It'd kill us if we got anywhere near it. It's the most horrible and disgusting plague juice ever devised."

"Is that right?" said the black magician. "Well, I bet you can't squirt *me*."

"Don't make it angry," begged his brother.

But that, of course, is just what the black magician wanted to do. He danced round it, shouting at it, calling it rude names and saying the kind of disgusting, wounding things only a black magician would know how to say. And the ant grew more and more furious and squirted out more and more plague juice. But the more furious it got the less accurate it became, until there was a huge pool of brown plague juice on the floor of the cell, but none at all on the black magician.

The ant started to feel a little groggy. It had managed to kill thousands and thousands of people and here was one horrible little human putting its thumb to its nose and saying the most awful scandalous things about him, the Head Ant, the Senior Spreader of Disease anywhere in the world.

He ran, or rather scuttled, towards the infuriating figure in front of him, his forelegs waving, his fleshy tap cocked for action. And the black magician stood, just in front of the pool of plague juice, grinning and jeering, as the ant lumbered towards him.

You can guess what happened, can't you?

Yes – at the last moment the black magician stepped neatly aside, and the Head Ant charged straight into the pool of plague juice. With a horrible scream, his forelegs crinkled like plastic pushed into fire and his two hundred eyes wept bloody tears, as if they had been drenched in acid. And that was the end of the Head Plague Ant.

"Now," said the black magician to his brother, "all we have to do is to bottle this stuff and squirt it at all the other ants."

"We have to get out of here first", said the white magician.

His brother grinned.

"When the king sees this", he said, pointing to the plague juice, "we will have no problem."

And they didn't. The two brothers were released from prison. They worked out a way of bottling the plague juice and both white and black magicians from all over the country came to help them. In a month, all the white ants were dead and the plague was no more. The king pardoned both the brothers (now firm friends as a result of working together on "Project Plague Juice", as it became known) and announced that from now on there was no such thing as black or white magic. In fact, all forms of magic were banned, and black and white magicians throughout the country turned to the really clever and interesting things that have helped to make the world a better place today – science and literature and art, all of which, if worked at and practised honestly and sincerely, and not for money or false glory, are the highest form of good thing you can do.'

I turned to them.

'That's the end of the story,' I said. 'And that's the point of the story, you see – and the point is the same as the point of any story, the Bible or the story of what happened to you today – the point is to show us how to live our lives better.'

They gazed at me, baffled by my sudden passion, my blatant moral harangue. They wanted more about ants.

'How doeth thith thtory,' said Paul, 'teach uth to live our liveth better?'

'Well,' I said, 'we have to work at what is in front of us. That's one thing. And we have to try and be responsible, about the things and people around us, from pebbles to brothers.'

'Was that story true?' said Sam.

'No,' I said. 'But I tried to make what it meant true.'

There was a silence in the car. Jane looked at me at last. She looked self-contained and yet unhappy. Very gently her hand reached out and nearly touched my arm.

'It's foo late,' she said. 'I'm sorry.'

The children were silent.

'I know,' I said.

TWENTY

'Woth the black magician good after that?' said Paul.

'He tried to be,' I said.

'And what happened to the white magician?' said Tom.

'He was all right,' I said. 'He lived happily. They all lived happily. In the end.'

They seemed puzzled. I had ended the story on too obvious a moral note. My mind wasn't on it. Or perhaps I'm revising the end. Giving it a moral I should have applied in my own life. As I said, I am not telling the story exactly as I told it. I can't quite remember the words I used: all I recall is that somebody or other was brave and good and the plague went away and it was as if there never had been any plague or pebble or meddling with the world.

Am I telling any of this *quite* as it happened? The story of what happened to me and the story I told my children – none of it happened as I have described it. I had a wife and now I didn't have one and I told my children a story and there was a pebble in it and somebody was good and somebody was bad but this is not how it was. Of course it isn't. What probably happened is that Paul asked for the story and I said there wasn't any more story. This was positively the last time I was telling the story and no it didn't have an end because life, like rivers, has no precise boundaries, merely an endless series of beginnings.

Well, this is the end of my story and I will try to tell it as it happened. I will try not to lie or to lean on magic, charms and prophecy.

I didn't fight for my wife. I think I realized, too late, that I did love her, but was too proud, perhaps, to put up a fight. I know we didn't row. We were as civilized as we had been that afternoon in the car when I finished my story. We were divorced later that year and Jane now lives with the man I continue to think of as Kevin. He sounds a right little Kevin on the telephone, caring and thoughtful and nice and non-sexist and anti-nuclear. Sometimes, when I've finished talking to him, I get the urge to go round and stick my fist in his face.

I don't, of course. I'm the kind of Englishman that doesn't like to make a fuss.

He asks me, continually, whether I want to see the *kids*. I don't think he's yet noticed that I put a slight emphasis on the word *children* when I'm talking to him. I tell him, continually, that I am too busy. It hurts me to be with them, you see, because, although I am not a caring anti-racist, non-nuclear post-feminist father, I do love them in my own way. I cannot bear the idea of their belonging to someone else. Which is why I am allowing them to become Kevin's children. Or, perhaps I should say, *Kevin's kids*.

My opera singer went back to New York. It turned out the man there was more serious than I had thought. It turned out, too, there were two men. And a few more in Canada besides. I don't miss her, but I find myself, from time to time, thinking nostalgically about her bottom. My business seems to run itself very well without me, and I spend most of my days here, in my clean new flat overlooking the Park, writing page after page, trying to make sense of what has happened. But it turns, as does everything else these days, into stories, stories that I cannot quite make sense of,

113

stories that have lost their magical power to change and instruct.

Just before I left for good, I took my three sons out to the river. I don't know where Jane was. With Kevin, I suppose. It was late summer. We were down by Teddington Lock, where the tidal Thames ends, sitting above the huge first lock, where the water is spread out like a tablecloth, fringed with a white weir of lace.

We were sitting in silence. I wasn't telling stories. I didn't tell them stories after that Spring, although they often asked me for them. I told them I was going away, but I tried to make it sound like a calm, rational decision. I would see them, I said, very, very often. And perhaps, when they are firmly and securely Kevin's children, I will see them. They need someone to love and it seems better to me that, in the words of that Sixties song, they should love the one they're with.

'Tell uth more about that withardth one,' said Paul, as we sat by the Thames.

'I can't,' I said. 'I'm sorry. I can't think of anything else that happened.'

'Tell uth it again then,' said Paul.

'Oh darling,' I said. 'I can't tell it. I can't.'

'You never tell uth thtorieth,'' he said. 'You never do.'

I couldn't answer that.

'Why are you going away?' he went on.

I found, to my horror, that I was crying. Paul came to me and wound himself into me. Then the other two added themselves and the three of them clung to me as I sobbed, ugly, disfiguring tears, as unstoppable as nausea, shaming, public tears, tears for my father, tears for the love I never worked hard enough to keep, tears for my own laziness and cowardice, tears for the way we all carry on to ourselves and others, tears for the future.

'I'm thorry,' said Paul.

He thought, you see, that I was crying because of what he had said about the story, that I was upset because I had no story to bring him.

'Thtorieth are hard to do thometimeth,' he said.

'Yes,' I said.

We lay there, on the bank, twined into each other. A little later, when I was myself again, we got up and walked on down the towpath. Sam stayed with me and the other two ran on ahead.

I watched them in the pale, sickly afternoon sun. They were the A Team, briefly. They stopped to examine a snail. They walked sideways for some way. Then they started a game called 'Chickenaboo'. Paul had to cry and his brother had to ignore him. If Paul convinced him his tears were real he gained a Chickenaboo point.

He gained several Chickenaboo points. He cried very convincingly.

Then the eldest boy came back to me and asked me several questions about X-rays. Paul wandered off on his own, ahead of us.

I noticed he was scanning the ground ahead of him. I thought, at first, that he was looking for snails, but, from time to time, he would drop to his knees and scrabble in the earth. Occasionally he would find something he seemed to think he wanted, but always rejected it. I couldn't see what he was collecting.

Then he found it. He stood up and, blonde head bent over it in concentrated study, brought it back to us.

He was closer than ten yards before I saw that what he was holding was a pebble. A perfect, round, grey pebble, as implacably itself as the object in my story. He went over to the river, dropped on to his belly, and washed the pebble in the stream. When he was sure it was clean he dried it on his T-shirt and ran back to me, clutching it. He held it up to me, squinting at the sickly sun as he tried to look into my eyes.

'It'th for you,' he said. 'It's a pebble.'

'Thankyou', I said.

My eldest son nodded.

'Good,' he said. 'Good.'

'Who knowth?' said Paul. 'Could be magic.'

'Who knows?' I said.

He continued to try to catch my eye.

'It'th a pwethent,' he said, 'becauth you're going away.'

'Thanks,' I said. I leaned down and kissed his small, pink-clenched lips.

'Maybe,' I said, 'when I touch it, I'll be able to summon you up. Like a genie.'

'Could be,' said Paul.

He let me kiss him one more time.

It's on my desk now as I write. It's funny but I hardly ever pick it up. Not that I'm superstitious: I don't imagine the three of them will suddenly arrive in front of me, demanding to be entertained, asking the impossible questions they ask me when I see them. Because I've never thought about it. Not until now, not until this moment, the moment that I write the word *pebble* in red ink on an empty white sheet of foolscap.

But now I have written the word I think maybe I'll touch the thing it describes. I look out across the park and reach my hand across the papers on my desk and close my fingers over the pebble as tightly as I would grasp one of my own children's hands, and I take full possession of it. It feels solid and perfect and unassailable. It's a beautiful thing, like so many things in the world, and, as I hold it close I seem to hold my lost children to me, as I had promised Paul that afternoon. They rise up before me in all their innocence and vulnerability, lights in a wicked world, and I put my arms around them the way I did that day by the river and feel once again that love you feel for children, hopeless, awkward, expressed at parting and greeting, waking and sleeping and too often forgotten between, until the moment of the last and final parting, too often soppy or stern or wound around with *must* and *should*, but always, when felt, uncomfortably close to tears.